'Bobbie Ann Cole has succeeded in telling … y of heart-rending times, told through … an innocently caught up in them … d Bobbie does it brilliantly. …
Michele Guinness, Author an…

'A moving story, evocative an… …'
Andrew Bartlett, author of Men … Christ: Fresh Light from the Biblical Texts

'An engaging story of identity and belonging in which a young girl must decide on her own future. Lena Levi's dilemma is written with great command and insight … A truly compelling read.'
Caroline Greville, Author of Badger Clan *and Lecturer in Creative Writing at Christ Church University, Canterbury*

'This is an assured novel with well-crafted characters and a ring of authenticity that left me wanting to find out more about Lena Levi's continuing life journey.'
Martyn Barr, Author of The Young Person's History Guide to Canterbury

'A fast-paced, brilliantly written tale of identity and history!'
Laura Fels, Deputy Director, Christian Embassy London

'The challenge of discovering Lena's true identity and coming to terms with the implications for this young woman's life are delightfully portrayed as she finds her way through confusion and anger to new discoveries about the fulness of life.'
Reverend Sara Bimson, Minor Canon, Canterbury Cathedral

'I loved this book. *Being Lena Levi* took me to some places and times which I needed to visit, and had not previously understood … This teenage girl's quest for identity and belonging in a broken world has much to say to our generation, and I'm looking forward to passing it on to my teenage daughter who I think will love it too!'
Dr Corinne Hagan, Pastor's Wife, Chair of Kent Women's Convention

'This gripping novel will take you on a journey into the real drama for many Holocaust survivors. It touched my heart with fresh compassion as the dramatic story unfolded. I recommend this moving novel as a true glimpse into one life story during this tumultuous time in history.'
Nancy Wilson, Author, Speaker, Global Ambassador for Cru, Orlando, USA

'Bobbie Ann Cole weaves an impressive narrative which explores issues of identity, belonging, family relationships and cultural dynamics. It is an enjoyable read which will appeal to many, and gives insights into the joys and struggles of Israeli life and finding what is meant by seeking to find "home".'
Rev Alex Jacob, CEO, The Church's Ministry among Jewish People

'The character-driven plot, combined with a narrative that draws you in, makes this a must-read book. Bobbie Ann Cole is a writer to watch.'
Wendy H Jones Award-winning Author and President of the Scottish Association of Writers

'*Being Lena Levi* is a faith story that needs to be told. As Lena finds her way through the relational complexities of having two mothers, she wrestles with her newly acquired Jewish history as it confronts the Christian faith of her upbringing. As Christians we have often ignored our rich and foundational Jewish heritage. Bobbie Ann Cole invites us to journey with Lena and discover the richness of Christ stepping out of the Jewish tradition. In embracing them both, we too find our way home to a fuller faith and deeper understanding of where we belong.'
Pastor Heidi Billington, NextGen Ministries, Smythe Street Church, Canada

Being Lena Levi

Bobbie Ann Cole

instant
apostle

First published in Great Britain in 2019

Instant Apostle
The Barn
1 Watford House Lane
Watford
Herts
WD17 1BJ

British Library Cataloguing-in-Publication Data

A catalogue record for this book is available from the British Library.

This book and all other Instant Apostle books are available from Instant Apostle:

Website: www.instantapostle.com

E-mail: info@instantapostle.com

ISBN 978-1-912726-09-7

Printed in Great Britain.

Dedication

For Tania, who loves Mutti

Acknowledgements

To me, England and Israel are like two beloved daughters – one quiet and gracious, the other fiery and unpredictable. In real life, I have only one daughter, Tania, who combines both personalities. I am grateful to her for her positivity, enthusiasm for my characters, encouragement and picky reading of my manuscript.

Others equally picky who have helped improve it vastly are Stephanie Nickel in Canada and Sheila Jacobs in England. My heartfelt thanks to them.

And to my dear husband, Butch, who is lovely at giving me space and an expert at padding around quietly.

PART ONE

Chapter One

ENGLAND, MAY 1950

Mum looked odd, kind of pasty, as she opened the front door. I slung my heavy, half-term satchel with my dirty sports kit in it onto the hall floor. I hung my panama hat and blazer on the coat stand as usual, but instead of heading for the kitchen with promises of supper, Mum tugged at the hem of my skirt, fiddled with my tie and plaits and looked me up and down.

I was filled with a kind of dread. 'What is it? What's going on?'

It was as if I woke her up. 'We have a visitor, dear.'

I followed her into the front room that we hadn't used since Peter's family from next door came for tea and mince pies last Christmas. The atmosphere was chilly, though it was a warm day.

A blur of red sweater rushed towards me with a cry that might have been pain or joy. Strong perfume wafted over me as a woman's arms grabbed me and I found myself pressed up against the soft flesh of her bosom. We remained glued together in the middle of the room. Beneath her perfume, the woman smelled of mothballs and overflowing ashtrays. Strands of her black hair tickled my nostrils.

Wondering whether I was supposed to hug the stranger back, I turned to Mum. The look on her face terrified me. I'd never thought of her as fragile before, but right then she looked like she might break into little pieces. Clearly, something serious was happening; I hadn't the remotest idea what.

'Lena,' the strange woman began to murmur. She said it Lay-Na, over and over.

No one ever called me Lena. Yet the sound of it took the bottom out of my belly and left a longing there I didn't understand, like someone strumming half-forgotten guitar chords that I loved. I pictured myself as in a dream, with my cheek on a big pillow soaked with tears, yearning to hear 'Lena'.

I winced under the stranger's scrutiny as she held me at arm's length. What was she hoping to see? Did I pass muster? Why should I even care?

Her eyes were brown and rimmed with streaks of mascara. Her hair was swept into a low bun. Her cherry-red lips matched her tight-fitting sweater. She was a young woman and beautiful, I thought – like a movie star, although her teeth were stained yellow from tobacco. Her smile lit up her whole face. I wanted to earn that smile again and again.

She pinched my cheek. 'Lena, *so gross geworden.*'

I didn't know how I understood what she said, but I knew it was German and that she was telling me I'd grown tall. Her face crumpled. She clasped me in another bear hug. Her body heaved. She wet my neck with her crying.

I turned to Mum and mouthed, 'Who is she?'

She flinched, which was not reassuring.

'Who is she?'

Mum looked desperate. Her lips moved, but no sound came from them. She cleared her throat and tried again. In a voice not her own, I heard her say, 'She's your mother.'

Her words made no sense. They bounced around the room and flew back off the walls at me like a volley of stinging arrows, without meaning. Yet they turned my blood ice-cold and my body clammy. I shouldered off the woman's suffocating embrace like she was a disease.

'No, she's not!' My throat was parched. The room was closing in. I squirmed. 'Let me go!'

Still she had my hands. I snatched them away. A jumble of husky words from her followed me as I lurched through the door. I caught a glimpse of Mum as I went. She looked afraid. I'd never seen her looking afraid before.

Fighting back the black that was engulfing me, I went out of the back door. I was panting like I'd just finished a cross-country run. I glanced behind me as I sucked in gulps of air but neither mother followed; a relief but also vaguely disappointing.

Mr Price next door was strutting around his back garden, smoke rising from his pipe in choo-choo puffs. If he saw me, he'd be bound to ask in his usual hearty way how 'we' were doing at school. I scooted down the garden, crouching below the level of the fence to avoid him.

The gardens in Lanfranc Close were long and narrow. At the end of ours was a great weeping willow tree with a bad hairdo, whose trailing tendrils masked an old bomb shelter. From the outside this looked like a hump of earth covered with balding grass. The steps down to the low opening where the door once was were overgrown with lilac and buddleia.

Inside was my very own fox's lair, the place where schools for dollies gave way to daydreams growing up. No one else except Mum knew this was here. And she never came. I sat on one of the concrete benches that ran along the two longer sides. With my knees hugged to my chest, I waited for my breath to calm, but it refused to do so. It was like I could see everyone in my school closing in on me out of the dark corners of the shelter, all whispering and pointing fingers.

I hugged my knees so tight that I felt I'd throw up. The crawling thing inside me felt like guilt, but I'd done nothing bad that I could think of.

The stranger had come like a flood that swept everything I thought I knew away, dragging off my identity and leaving me without a rock to cling to. I had no past, no future and no answers, only questions. If she really was my mother, why had she left me here? What kind of a mother would abandon her daughter like that?

Come to think of it, what kind of a mother was the woman I called Mum? She always said honesty was the best policy. But, for all this to be true, she'd had to have told me a whopper big enough to turn my whole life into a made-up story. After all, it wasn't possible to have two mothers. Only one of them could be real. Right? But which one? The one who'd dumped me or the one who'd lied to me? Right then, I wanted nothing to do with either of them.

A breath of wind came down the stairs, cooling the tears running hot down my cheeks. I glanced up to see if one of them had come. But no. Both had left me all alone. Well, I had nothing to say to either of them anyway.

The new mother's eyes were half-moon shaped and brown, like mine. Mum's were grey, like a cloudy sky, like her hair. Mum was too old to have a daughter of fourteen and a half. But the other one was too young.

I wondered how I'd understood her German. I was in the Latin stream at school and had never learned German. Yet, as I bolted, she'd said, '*Du weisst wohl wer Du bist*.' And I knew what that meant: 'You know very well who you are.'

Well, she was wrong about that. I had no idea.

Chapter Two

Mum was in the garden, calling, 'Marlene, are you there? Supper's ready.'

I heard her but didn't react. When the words had finally sunk in, I scrambled out of the bomb shelter and ran past her, through the back door and into the house. The front room was empty. The Other Mother was gone, leaving only her bittersweet smell behind.

Panic rose in me. 'Where is she?'

The woman had no sticking power. And no consideration for my feelings. Clearly, she hadn't considered that I might be hurt by her abandonment, which would be glaring to anyone with a modicum of compassion. There was more – much more – I needed to know.

I tramped into the back room and sat down at the square table with a sigh. I didn't want to ask Mum anything. Mum could no longer be trusted. She brought us plates of baked beans on toast. We both behaved as if I hadn't yelled.

She said, 'For what we are about to receive…'

And I cut in, 'Amen.'

It was like nothing had happened and my life hadn't been ripped to shreds, though I found I couldn't swallow, even though I was ravenous. Eyes brimming with tears, I watched Mum eat. She knew I was watching but carried on, saying nothing.

Her hair tamed by grips, her wrap-around apron and her pearly clip-on earrings all confirmed a no-nonsense attitude. To her, right was white, wrong was black, and she followed the path of truth. Yet she'd cruelly deceived me.

My vision misted. I looked towards the clock on the mantelpiece that was ticking away the seconds. I wished I could get up, open its glass front, and turn back the hands to ordinary, to arriving home from school and ringing the doorbell again, to hanging up my things and thoughts of supper, to her not saying, 'We have a visitor, dear.'

Mum lay her knife down beside her fork. She turned to me with an extra-kind expression on her face that jabbed another ice pick of alarm into my heart. 'This is hard for you, Marlene, I know. Please understand that it's hard for me too...'

The sneer I intended came out as a sob. She was going to tell me something I didn't want to hear, and I had to let her. Though I wanted to run, I didn't. Though the buzzing of a whole hive of bees in my brain was setting my teeth on edge, I listened.

'It's hard too, for... Mutti,' she said.

'Is that her name?' My mouth was dry again. It was hard to get the words out.

'Her name is Mrs Levi, Rochel Levi.' She pronounced it Rock-el. 'We would say Rachel, I think. And Mutti is...'

'... *Mum* in German.'

The image that flickered before my mind's eye didn't match the sweet sound of that word at all. The oom-pah-

pah of a sliding trombone would describe it better. I was watching from the wings of a darkened theatre as a woman with cherry-red lips, like the stranger's, sang and danced behind eerie green footlights. She had on black stockings and a top hat. The scene brought the crawlies back into my belly and I didn't know why. Perhaps it was because I was absolutely sure at that moment that Mrs Rochel Levi was my mother.

I jumped up and backed away, drowning in a sea of hurt that caused actual pain behind my eyes, in my throat and down my spine. At the same time, it was like a hand was squeezing my heart hard enough to drain the blood from it. 'Why didn't you tell me?'

'Sit down, dear.' Mum's voice was firm, though her face was ashen. She patted the seat.

I shook my head. I was feeling like bolting again. Yet, at the same time, I was glued where I stood.

'You knew,' she said.

'No, I didn't! *You* were my mother. But it turns out you're a... an... imposter.'

She winced.

I jabbed my finger at her. 'Who are you?'

'You don't remember?'

'Remember what?'

'The *Kindertransport*.'

More German! 'What's that?'

She patted the chair again. 'Sit down and I'll explain.'

I took a step forward. I had to know. But I sat with my knees sideways on, in case I needed a fast getaway.

With a deep sigh, Mum began. 'It was a grey November day at the beginning of the winter before the war started –

1938. I was baking a Victoria sponge and listening to the Home Service on the wireless…'

In a flash, I was right there with her, remembering the old farmhouse kitchen where we used to live and its yeasty bread smell. I would stand on black slate tiles beside a long table, high as my nose, as she sifted flour into a big bowl.

'They broadcasted a call for foster parents to come forward, for the children who were coming,' she went on. 'You see, Hitler, the German leader…'

'I know who Hitler was, Mum!' The word 'Mum' felt furry in my throat. Perhaps I shouldn't call her that any more?

'Hitler and his Nazi Party were making life unbearable for the Jews in Germany.' She looked at me as if she were expecting this to strike a chord. She was wrong. I glared back at her.

Hesitantly, she went on. 'He stirred up all the other Germans until everyone hated the Jews. On Crystal Night they smashed up the Jewish shop windows and beat up the owners. It was a scary time. Your mother would have feared more and more for your safety, and her own.'

I hated it when she said 'your mother'. It was like motherhood was something you could just transfer over to someone else. And the thought that I wasn't who I thought – that nothing was solid any more – left a taste like cold metal in my mouth. 'If she's my mother now, then you're not responsible for me any more. Are you? I don't have to do what you say.'

My sneer missed its mark. Mum only looked like she felt sorry for me. My mind was racing on. If she – Mutti – was Jewish, perhaps I was too. But they were the unfortunates you pitied because of the hatred that had been shown them. I had thought I was properly British, part of a proud nation that ruled the waves, whose vast dominions coloured the world map pink.

It all seemed so unreal. When I tried to remember Germany and being Jewish, what came at me out of the floaty fog were vague snapshots from the time before Mum and I moved here to Canterbury: her hauling me aboard the tractor she was driving, letting me help feed chickens and bring in bleating sheep. We used to have a farm in Wales where the grass was as green as the tiny glass of crème de menthe Mum would sip at Christmas.

'Over here, we thought all that was very wrong,' she said. 'Britain agreed to take 10,000 Jewish children. You didn't all come at once but in dribs and drabs.'

'So, *I* am Jewish!'

'Why, yes, dear.'

'They don't believe in Jesus!'

'That's right.'

'Will they still allow me in the church?'

'Of course. Jesus Himself was Jewish.'

'He was?'

She smiled. 'And the disciples and almost everyone else in the Bible.'

'I've heard 6 million Jews died in the war,' I said.

She nodded. 'It was good that you came to England.'

Perhaps some of them were my uncles and aunts, cousins or grandparents. I'd heard about the concentration camps where they murdered Jews in gas chambers. At Auschwitz, the biggest and most well-known camp, they had a sign over the gate that said in German: *Work Sets You*

Free. That was nothing but a big lie to help the Nazis keep everybody under control. Those who weren't gassed were worked to death on starvation rations, never mind if they were sick or old, or were children.

My hand flew to my mouth. Perhaps it would have been my own fate to die that way if I'd stayed... But maybe not. That woman who'd said she was my mother and then vanished had got through. No doubt I would have too.

I cut into the sober silence that had fallen. 'Six million is a massive number.'

'Yes.'

I leaned forward. 'Go on, then.'

'I talked to Daddy and we decided we'd apply.'

On the bureau sat the framed photograph of a handsome man in his forties wearing the uniform of a naval lieutenant. I had no memories of him of my own, but it was like I did because Mum never stopped talking about the wonderful person he was. That picture was like a holy relic to her. And so, also, to me.

Now everything was shifting. He was as much a stranger as my real father. A thought hit me like a brick. Perhaps my real father had been murdered in the camps.

'Someone came to inspect our home and interview us. And we were approved.' Mum smiled to herself, no doubt remembering the sweet day in her sweet life that approval arrived.

I narrowed my eyes, wondering what other secrets there might be. 'You never had any other children? I mean, children of your own?'

'No. We just didn't.' She shook her head. Looking right at me, she went on, 'We thought we were doing something good for a refugee child, but I was very glad to have you when Daddy was away fighting, and even more so after the news came that he'd been killed.'

'Daddy?' Claws of bitterness had gripped my vocal chords.

Mum, who wasn't the soppy, sentimental sort, surprised me then by reaching for my hand and squeezing it. 'You came with a little suitcase. There wasn't much inside. No winter clothes. But then, we didn't know how long you'd be staying. It was supposed to be a temporary thing. But we sort of connected. Didn't we?'

I stayed cold, remembering the terrible lie she'd let us live, though I was beginning to realise that I was mostly angry because I desperately wanted her to be my real mother and she never would be again. No amount of fiddling with the clock hands could change that now that the truth was out. Mum didn't seem to care that I'd turned to wood.

I couldn't stand it any more. I got up and headed for the kitchen. When I got there, I was at a loss as to what to do with myself. The back door and the shelter at the end of the garden beckoned. But I had a need to know everything, although I dreaded what else she might say. After a moment's hesitation, I filled a glass with water and took it straight back to the back room. Mum looked relieved.

'So, what did happen at the end of the war?' I was asking to hear something sweet – hoping she'd say she loved me too much to let me go – yet my voice was as sharp as a shard of glass.

Again, she sighed deeply. 'You *Kindertransport* children were all supposed to go back to where you came from. But that was impossible. Most of you had no one left to go back to. Whole families had been wiped out.'

'But not my… mother?'

'When no one claimed you, I assumed that was what had happened to your people.'

'And that I'd stay with you?'

'And that you'd stay with me.' She reached for my hand again.

I was having none of it. This was all her fault. It was like she'd kidnapped me and I was her hostage. I jumped to my feet. 'You're mean, Mum! All these years you've kept me in the dark. You've denied me my rightful identity. You've kept me from my true mother.'

No matter that I wasn't sure my rightful identity was something I wanted. Or that I found the colourful woman claiming to be my mother a little scary. Right at this minute, all I wanted was to get away from Mum and the gloomy little world she'd cocooned me in under false pretences. All this upset was down to her, 100 per cent her fault. 'I hate you!'

I stormed out of the room and upstairs to my bedroom. I threw myself onto my bed and reached for One-Eyed Lottie. She was the rag doll I'd had forever. She had brown woollen plaits, black knitted shoes and a grubby red woollen pinafore. Once my dearest plaything, now that I was big, she mostly sat on my bed all day. I cuddled her close.

After what seemed like a long time, Mum's footsteps creaked on the stairs. When she stood in the doorway, I turned my face to the window, which, being a warm afternoon, was open. The voice of Doris Day singing

'Bewitched, Bothered, and Bewildered' was drifting in from one of the dorms of the boarding school at the end of the garden.

'I suppose I should have tried to find out what became of your family when the war ended,' she said. 'But you never asked, and I was content not to pursue something that might ultimately cause you distress and force you to choose.'

How could she be so matter-of-fact? 'You make me sick,' I said under my breath. I'd never cheeked her this way before. It made me feel bad even though she deserved it.

Mum chose to ignore my words. 'Marlene, poor Mrs Levi. The hotel is expensive. I'm sure she wants to get to know you. And you must...'

'Must what?'

'You must want to get to know her.'

'No!' I scooted my whole body to face the window, away from her.

Though I was eaten up with curiosity, I dreaded what might come out. I was getting a memory, maybe...

The dream-like picture of the cabaret dancer with cherry-red lips was returning. This time, a little version of me was there. I was feeling as anxious as before. I saw myself, trying to get to her. But giant hands lifted me. A grey-haired man in a brown overall – a stagehand, perhaps – put me back in the wings. I had to stay right where I was, he said, though I needed the toilet so badly. 'Mutti!' I cried in desperation as hot wee surged into my knickers and dribbled down my leg. Her head half-turned in my direction, but she kept her fixed smile and carried on with her act, leaving me shivering in my shame.

'Perhaps we should ask her to stay with us?' Mum was saying.

'What?'

I didn't like this idea at all. My protests, however, were feeble. Though I hadn't asked for any of this, there seemed no other way to try to unravel the mystery of who I really was.

I trailed after her to the phone box at the end of the road. We called the place where the Mutti was staying. I was surprised when they held a conversation: Mutti was clearly responding to Mum's English. They agreed she would come to stay tomorrow and see how things went.

'Perhaps it'll be a nice day for a picnic,' Mum said, as we walked home.

Her suggestion sounded so normal. I wondered how she could remain calm when I was a million miles from getting used to what was going on. Tomorrow held the prospect of long hours spent with a mother I didn't know and wasn't sure I wanted to.

Tomorrow would be worse even than today.

Chapter Three

First thing the following morning, I hurried next door to Peter's. Mrs Price went upstairs to wake him while I waited in the hall with my hands clasped together in front of me to hide my body from Mr Price in his dressing gown and pyjamas. 'You look very attractive in those shorts, Marlene,' he said.

It was a sunny morning. I'd put on my flowered cotton top and blue shorts. On my feet were my plimsolls. I wished I was waiting outside, and not only because of the sun.

'How's that beautiful mother of yours?'

My heart surged. I thought for a moment he knew my secret. Then I realised he meant Mum and not the Other Mother. 'Very well, thank you.'

'Doing anything exciting over the Whitsun holiday?'

'Uh-uh.' I wasn't about to tell him anything about anything.

Peter appeared at the top of the staircase in striped pyjamas, rubbing his eyes. What a relief.

'Can you come out?' I said.

'I'll be right there.' He turned and disappeared. He was true to his word. I was standing waiting for no time at all.

'Be good.' Mr Price chuckled as he opened the door to let us out. 'And if you can't be good, be careful.'

I was too polite not to say goodbye to a grown-up. But the door shut as I turned. So, I was glad I didn't have to.

'What's up?' Peter asked.

I took him to the bomb shelter.

'Wow! This is a keen place.' He went down the steps and bent to go through the doorway. This last month or two he'd shot up several inches. He was stretching like an elastic band. 'It's like a smaller version of the shelter we had at school. But that was stinky, with a bucket behind a rag of curtain for a toilet. How come you never mentioned this be–'

'Never mind. Sit down.'

We sat on the concrete bench. I swore him to secrecy. 'And may God's thunderbolt strike me dead if I ever tell another living soul what Marlene is about to tell me,' I made him repeat, holding his hand to his heart. When he'd finished he looked me in the eye. 'That promise only holds if I'm sure you won't come to harm through whatever is going on.'

'OK.'

I told him everything. Afterwards he was silent. The birds were twittering and a squirrel was chattering. I could hear the low murmur of conversation from the boys' dormitories beyond the back fence.

'What are you going to do?' he asked, eventually.

'No idea. I was hoping you'd have a suggestion.'

'There's a Bible story about a child with two mothers.'

'There is?'

I'd never heard of it, but then, he was more churchy than I was. He went to Bible study and was a youth leader. It didn't seem to bother him in the least when others teased him and called him a goody-goody.

'They go to King Solomon, both claiming the child is theirs.'

'And?'

'Solomon asks for a sword to cut the child in two.'

'Well, that's a bit drastic!'

I was seeing myself tied up like in the old silent movies, with a sharp-toothed rotary saw bearing down on me.

Peter grinned. He had a charming grin. 'That's not the end of the story. The real mother backs down.'

'She does?'

Would my real mother, the Mutti, back down? If she did, then nothing in my life would change. I could stop chewing my nails. Maybe they'd actually grow, and I could paint them shocking pink, like my best friend, Babs. But would that mean my life would turn out to be a big disappointment? Would I be stuck here in Lanfranc Close forever?

Just yesterday at school, Miss MacGrotty had invited my class to consider our futures. I had wished mine would turn out more exciting than the routine of school and home and church on Sundays that was stifling my adventurous spirit.

She asked us what career appealed. This was to help us think about subject choices for the new GCE O level public examination course we would be starting in September. She handed out cards for us to write on. As I watched girls outside the window pounding the track in navy knickers, no ideas came. My blank card looked up at me reproachfully.

I later shared my dilemma with Peter, after running into him walking home from school.

'So, what did you put down in the end?' He had to raise his voice above the noise of the buses and cars passing us, as we ambled towards Canterbury's imposing Westgate Towers, once the main gate to London in the medieval city walls.

'Er… farmer.'

'Farmer?' He snorted with laughter.

My cheeks burned. I glued my eyes to the pavement, feeling silly. I soon had to raise them to squeeze past throngs of American tourists, exclaiming at our timbered houses and 'seventeenth-century' witches' ducking stool.

Farmer was an odd choice, I supposed, for someone who lived a bookish sort of a life in the centre of a bustling city like Canterbury.

'Sorry, Marlene.' Peter looked concerned. 'That wasn't very nice of me. I have no idea what I want to be.'

'The farmer idea was desperate,' I conceded. 'I had to write something.'

I glanced back at the tourists with their cameras. They took home snaps of what they wanted to see, I supposed, the towering medieval cathedral and the quaint houses from across the centuries, rather than the picket-fenced bomb sites that were like gaping teeth between them – a doorway leading nowhere, a single wall with a window in it, or a crater pushing up purple buddleia.

'Maybe you could marry a farmer?'

'Because girls can't be farmers?'

'I was thinking that a farm probably needs two people to run it.'

I hadn't replied. He was the one I wanted to marry.

'Solomon realised that the real mother loved the child enough to give it up,' Peter was saying.

If Mutti had really loved me, she'd have come way before now. The war ended five years ago. What took her so long?

'So, he gave her the child.'

'What? Solomon gave the real mother the child?'

'Yes.'

I tried to make the best of it. I clapped my hands. 'That's really keen.'

I didn't sound very convincing.

'Which mother will you choose?'

'Choose?'

Mum had used that word last night. I'd had the heebie-jeebies ever since.

'*Choose* rhymes with *lose*,' I said, like I was joking. Choosing wrong could ruin my life. Even choosing right would be awful. There could be no avoiding someone getting hurt.

Peter looked concerned. 'I'd like to pray for you.'

'Oh. Alright.'

Right there and then he laid a hand on my shoulder, closed his eyes, and prayed that God would give me the wisdom of King Solomon. I kept my eyes open. Even so, I felt it was nice. But the tingling silence after his 'amen' was too intense. I had to break it. 'Perhaps I won't even be allowed to choose. Perhaps the Other Mother has a legal claim and I'll just have to put up with what she decides.'

He shrugged.

'I suppose Solomon represents the powers that be in this world.' I pulled a wry face.

'I think Solomon represents you.'

Whatever I decided, if I got to decide at all, would cut me in two.

I went indoors after Peter went home. A green canvas suitcase was standing in the hallway. It was battered and covered in stickers, some of which had funny writing on them, not our alphabet at all.

My heart became lead. 'She's here?'

Mum was overly jolly. 'I've made a picnic lunch.'

I loved picnics. Sometimes we'd go to the Westgate Gardens. The River Stour running through this park was clear in summer: you could see green weed wafting in the water's flow, and fish swimming. These lovely gardens lay beside the old Westgate Towers, through which pilgrims once poured, hopeful of a miracle at the shrine of Thomas Becket in the cathedral. Another favourite of mine at the opposite end of the city was the Dane John Gardens with its lawns and avenue of lime trees. However, I liked wandering off into the country best of all, such as to Fordwich, an ancient village not far from Canterbury. You could sit in a grassy meadow beside the Stour there, with the woods at your back and an old hump-backed bridge beside an olde worlde pub in front of you.

The Other Mother appeared at the top of the stairs. Mum and I looked up and she made her grand entrance, with her perfume descending ahead of her. She was more composed than yesterday, wearing a big smile. Her hair, held back from her face by a stretchy headband, fell loose about her shoulders. And she was wearing slacks! I thought only movie stars wore those. They were stone coloured and hugged her figure, showing the sway of her hips as she came down the stairs.

Ignoring Mum, she took my hands in hers. 'Lena, you are so beautiful.'

My attempt at a smile froze on my face. She made me very nervous.

Inevitably, she pulled me to her and held me tight. Just like the previous day I managed not to flinch, though my arms remained wooden at my sides. I was feeling as much resentment towards her as I was towards Mum. They were both causing me a lot of upset.

The picnic turned out to be just her and me. I was furious with Mum when she told me she wasn't coming. My first urge was to storm off. My second was to shout and stamp my feet. The reason I did neither was that the Other Mother was clapping her hands in glee and saying, 'Vot a lovely idea,' in her strongly accented, raspy voice. 'Zis vill be fun, Lena.'

Now we were walking through the woods in silence. I was carrying the Red Riding Hood willow basket with all the food in it and feeling like the wolf might jump out of the shadows at us at any moment. To say I was on edge would be an understatement. I was a big disappointment to myself. I'd wished my life could be more exciting. Now, suddenly, it was, and I was miserable and unable to cope.

She tugged her cardigan across her shirt. 'It's cold.'

Although it was shady under the trees, the sunlight was filtering through the beech leaves and dappling the woodland floor. It wasn't cold at all. 'Are you ill?'

'*Nein.*' She stopped to light a cigarette, sucked on it hard and blew smoke out, over me.

I waved it away pointedly and coughed. 'That's very bad for you.'

'Life is bad for you.' She laughed. 'Actually, it's terminal.'

'You're a card. Aren't you?'

'Card?' She didn't even realise I was being sarcastic.

'Oh, come on.'

She followed me along the path. 'I'm used to the weather in Israel. It's hot. At least most of the time it is. We had fifteen centimetres of snow last January. I could not believe it.'

'Israel?' This was a revelation. 'I thought you lived in Germany.'

She laughed long and hard at this. 'Such an idea. No, I don't believe I'll ever go back there.'

I knew nothing about Israel beyond what I'd been taught in RE at school. I told myself I'd better smarten up and learn about this. It could turn out I'd be going to live there.

Squiggles of fear mingling with a weird kind of thrill wriggled in my belly at that alarming thought. The Pathé News at the cinema often talked about the war between the Jews and the Arabs in Israel – soldiers in helmets and tanks in the desert. Who would want to live there?

'Do you live in the desert?' Perhaps she lived near where Jesus was when He wandered for forty days and nights, tempted by the devil.

'No, I live on a kibbutz near Haifa.'

I didn't know what a kibbutz was and had never heard of Haifa.

'Haifa is a big port on the Mediterranean, in the northern part of the country. The kibbutz lies between there and Nazareth.'

'Where Jesus grew up?'

She frowned at me like I'd said a dirty word.

'Have you been to Nazareth?' I asked.

'Naturally. It's really near.'

'What's it like?' I imagined a pretty, historic village, probably a bit like Fordwich, where we were headed.

'Jews need to be careful there. There are many Arabs.'

'And the Arabs don't like the Jews?'

'Right.'

I wondered whether there were Christians there but thought I'd better not ask.

'What's Israel like?'

She thought about this for a moment. 'Israel is hope.'

How could a country be hope? I'd expected her to say something about the sights – there would be loads of biblical ones – or the scenery, or the weather. If someone asked me what England was like, I might say it's a 'green and pleasant land'. These were words from the song 'Jerusalem', which, oddly enough, is about England.

Her thoughts were turning towards a song too. Her eyes glowed. 'In *Hatikvah,* the national anthem, we sing about our hope to live in freedom in a land that belongs to us.

You see, Lena, we had no country when Hitler came against us, nowhere we could run to.'

I was burning to ask her about the Holocaust, about my family and my father, but I held back. That conversation didn't seem to fit with strolling along a woodland path with birds chirping in the trees above us.

'What about Bethlehem? Have you been there?'

Again, that no-entry sign frown. It stopped me dead from asking her if she'd seen Jesus' birthplace.

'Bethlehem is close to Jerusalem,' she said. 'But it's in Jordan.'

I'd never heard of Jordan. 'So, have you been?'

She stopped and stamped on her cigarette until it was quite dead. 'Are you a Christian, Lena?'

'Of course.' I stuck out my chest defiantly.

'The Nazis were Christians,' she snarled, and strode away.

I had to run to catch up with her. 'Maybe so. But not all Christians are Nazis. I'm not. Mum's not. Peter next door is not.'

I was surprised to see her face crumple. She threw her hands up in the air. 'I shouldn't have let you come here. Ach! But you couldn't stay with me either. You would be dead too.'

I wondered who she meant by 'too' – my father, perhaps? She looked like she might start howling. I hoped she wouldn't. I'd never had to deal with a grown-up in that state before. Luckily, she'd calmed down by the time we reached Fordwich meadow and sat down for our picnic.

I set out the tablecloth and the food Mum had put in the basket for us. There were Cheddar cheese and pickle sandwiches, some of Mum's special home-made sausage rolls, and a pork pie. She must have been hoarding our meat ration coupons. There was a bar of chocolate and lemonade. It was a feast.

'So,' I said.

She reached for a sandwich, took a bite and scrunched up her face. '*Schrecklich*!' She put down the triangle of white bread, which now had a lipstick-edged bite taken out of it, on the red-and-white checked tablecloth.

We hadn't yet said grace. I closed my eyes. 'For what we are about to receive, may the Lord make us truly thankful. Amen.'

I opened my eyes. Hers were closed. Perhaps she was praying, although no 'amen' had come from her.

'Um...' I didn't know how to address her. 'What should I call you? Should I call you Mutti?' The name felt gluey in my mouth.

She opened her eyes. They were deep and brown and lovely. She shrugged. 'What do you call her?'

'You mean Mum?'

'You can call me Mutti – or Imma.'

'Imma?'

'It's Hebrew for mother. Or Rochel.'

'That's your Christian name?'

'First name.'

I decided to move away from name choices for now. 'How old are you?' It was a cheeky question, but she was so young. She made Mum seem so old.

To my surprise, she answered me. 'I'm thirty.'

'But I'm fourteen and a half!' That would have made her just fifteen or sixteen when she had me.

A what-can-you-do look that left me none the wiser was her only response.

A bottle-green car, coming from the village, was crossing the narrow, hump-backed bridge over the River Stour, not far from where we were sitting. A second car approached, travelling in the opposite direction. There was only enough space for one car at a time. So, the green car backed up and, tucking in at the start of the bridge, allowed the other car to pass. The drivers waved to one another courteously. Again, the first car started to cross the bridge. The same thing happened again. On its third try, the green car stayed where it was, forcing the car coming from the other direction to back up. We exchanged grins. It was an amusing pantomime.

'Mutti.' My throat constricted. The name felt too big. 'Would you like a piece of pork pie?'

'Jews don't eat pork.' Her tone implied this was obvious.

In my hand I had one of Mum's sausage rolls. She made them with shortcrust pastry and spread ketchup between the meat – mixed with breadcrumbs to help eke it out – and the pie crust. They were totally delicious. I didn't feel Jewish. But if I was the Mutti's daughter, then I must be. So, should I eat it? Or not?

It didn't take long to decide I should. I reasoned I'd been eating Mum's sausage rolls all my life.

The Mutti hated cheese with pickle. She wouldn't touch pork. She casually picked up our solitary chocolate bar and scoffed it, as if sweets weren't rationed at all.

Wasps began to annoy us. I put everything except the tablecloth back in the picnic basket. We sat in the sunshine watching the weeds waving in the river. Several times, I opened my mouth to speak and shut it again. There was so much I wanted to ask about how we used to be, but I didn't know where to start. So, I tried to keep it conversational. 'What do you do for a living?'

'I told you. I live on a kibbutz.'

'What's a kibbutz?'

'We have kibbutzim all over Israel. We live together and work together and share everything.'

'Who does?'

'The kibbutznikim.'

'Pardon?'

She sighed like I was a bit dense. 'That's what people who live on all the kibbutzim are called. It sounds Russian, doesn't it? And it is.' She flicked her hair out of her eyes as the breeze caught it. 'It's a Russian type of system, a sort of communism.'

Well! I wondered how she could speak lightly of communism. Only countries we didn't get along with were communist. In communist countries everyone had to do the same and be the same, which, looking at the Mutti, didn't sound like her cup of tea at all.

But then she told me something about her life on the kibbutz. 'I get a full Israeli breakfast every day. We have our own hens and dairy cattle. We are lucky to have eggs and cheese. We have fruit and olives and cucumber and, of course, bread.'

'You have all that for breakfast?' Coming, as I did, from a childhood of wartime rationing, the breakfast sounded out of this world.

'We take what we want.'

I'd never eaten an olive. It sounded Mediterranean and exotic, something from far-off places with year-round warm climates.

'For lunch we have soup and meat and salads and dessert. There's supper too. Or I can take some things from the kibbutz shop. I don't have to pay.'

'You don't have to pay?'

She laughed. 'I take what I need – shampoo, cigarettes, clothes; chocolate, even, sometimes – whatever we have, when we have it.'

'Golly!'

It sounded too good to be true. I wondered if she was making it up.

'On Shabbat, we get together for songs and dancing.'

'What's Shabbat?'

'What do you call it? Ach, yes! Sabbath, the day of rest.'

I nodded. 'Sunday.'

'From sundown Friday to sundown Saturday,' she corrected, sounding a little peeved. '*Du bist keine Jüdin!*'

It sounded like she was accusing me of not being Jewish. She was being unreasonable. How could I be expected to know what being Jewish added up to?

'Of course, we don't get paid much. As good as nothing, really. But we have a roof over our heads and everything we can need. We are building a homeland for the Jewish people.' She looked at me and smiled. 'Perhaps you will join us?'

Was she serious, or was this a tease, a dangling carrot she might yank away so she could laugh at me? Would it even be possible for me to go to Israel? Did I dare? Did I want to? If I did, would it turn out to be an opportunity, or a curse?

'Don't you want adventure, Lena?'

I couldn't answer her. It was all so confusing. So, I shrugged helplessly. I wondered what was really going on here. She seemed to be playing some cat-and-mouse game.

Her eyes took on a dreamy look. Maybe this was just how she was – kind of foreign and overblown. 'After the work, on a summer's evening, we all get in the truck and drive to the beach. Swimming in the sea is a fun change from our swimming pool.'

'You have a swimming pool?'

'Of course.' She spoke as if everybody had one. 'We built it ourselves.'

'It sounds super.'

A silence fell between us. I hurried to fill it. 'It sounds just like Butlin's.'

'What's that?'

'It's a holiday camp. My best friend, Babs, is there right now.'

Yesterday she'd ducked behind the lid of her desk during English class to dab powder on her nose and tell me about her holiday plans. 'My dad's filling the car up. We're going to stay at Butlin's.'

It made no odds to me that petrol was coming off rationing. We didn't have a car. But I was impressed to hear she was going to Butlin's, which was for rich people. I tried not to sound envious. 'Have fun.'

Babs had responded with a wink that clearly I was supposed to understand but didn't.

'The kibbutz is no holiday camp,' the Mutti said. 'We must work.'

'What do you do?' If you'd asked me to guess, I might have said she worked in the kitchen, or maybe the shop. But no.

'I look after the cattle. I milk cows. I take them out to the field and guard them.'

To my surprise, she mimed wielding a rifle. I supposed that was in case they were stolen. They must have a lot of crime in Israel. Probably too, there were wild animals. When I used to attend Sunday school, we'd learned that King David, as a shepherd boy, practised long and hard with a sling, to protect his sheep from beasts like mountain lions and wolves. This gave him the skills he needed to take on the giant Goliath.

The Mutti's work wasn't vastly different from what Mum did in the war. But she was so elegant. I couldn't imagine her in dungarees and a headscarf like Mum used to wear.

'In the war, my mum used to look after sheep.' I thought I was making a connection between us, but the words 'my mum' seemed to hang in the air like a wedge. I soldiered on regardless. 'But I don't think we have to stand guard over our livestock here.'

Just then the fields all around Canterbury sounded like maternity wards, full of bleating lambs and their mothers. All without a farmer in sight, most of the time.

'I also give the little ones their bottles,' she went on. 'And I clean up the poo...'

She smirked at my disapproval of her bluntness and tapped yet another cigarette from her packet. It was almost empty. Her fingers were stained yellow from nicotine. She made me feel how Babs sometimes did, like a square. I didn't want to be a square. I wanted to wear slacks and lipstick.

The Mutti dragged on her cigarette. 'I send them off to where they are…' She mimed cutting her throat.

'The slaughterhouse?'

She laughed and gave a little wave. 'Bye-bye.'

Nastiness was batting between us like a ping-pong ball. How had our conversation turned so unpleasant? I searched for something to say – anything. 'You don't like your work?'

'We are building a country,' she replied. 'It's better than starving. Better than the gas chamber.'

It was like I was being made to feel guilty for the things I'd escaped; terrible things, no doubt, that I couldn't even begin to imagine.

Chapter Four

The ruby-red Sunday dress Mum had sewn me swished around my legs and made me feel pretty as I walked home from church with Peter the next day. We dawdled some way behind Mum and his parents as I told him about the picnic.

He seemed to know all about kibbutzes. 'They welcome young people from all over the world to work with them, helping out with fruit picking, or maintenance, or whatever. I could come out to your kibbutz and work for the summer, when I'm a bit older.'

I stopped and stared at him, feeling cornered by his plans. 'Who says I'm going to Israel?'

'A kibbutz would be a great place to learn farming.'

'Are you trying to get rid of me?'

'Don't you want to be a farmer any more?'

A lump came to my throat. A lot had happened since I'd told him that.

Embarrassed, I kept my eyes down as we followed an erratic path that ran beside the Stour. Here, the river constituted a moat alongside what was once the city wall. Bits of the old wall had been incorporated here and there into a row of Victorian houses.

On the water, two male mallard ducks were flapping their wings at each other, having an argument. These ducks often formed threes, with two green-headed males and one plain brown female. They would seem to get along for a while, and then not.

'It'll be alright, Marlene.' He eyed me closely as we walked. A grin spread across his face.

I could see no reason to smile. 'How can you say that? How would you know?'

He looked taken aback. 'I was only trying to help.'

I relented. 'I know.'

We rounded the corner into Lanfranc Close. The houses on our street were 1930s semis dressed up as Tudor mansions with dark beams across their whitewashed frontages. At the end of the street was a circle, covered in lilac bushes, where we had played when I was younger.

'Anyway, isn't Israel at war?' I said. 'Why would you want me to go and live in a country at war?'

'The War of Independence is over. Most of the Arab countries in the area have signed an armistice.'

'How do you know all this stuff?'

'I listen to the news. Don't you?'

'Not very often. And I've never taken much of an interest in Israel.'

'Of all the countries in the world, Marlene! Israel is the Holy Land.'

'I can't understand why the Mutti would choose to go and live there. She's not a bit interested in holy anything.'

'Think about it. It's the Jewish homeland.'

'Why couldn't she come and live here?' That way both mothers would be handy.

'She has no connection to here, but she does have a connection to Israel. You should read your Bible – Exodus. God gave Israel to the Jewish people. But they lost the land under the Roman occupation and were scattered. For nearly 2,000 years, they had to keep moving on because nobody wanted them.'

'Why?'

'I don't know. Maybe because they're different.'

'She is, I can tell you.' The Mutti was very different from anyone I'd ever met. I hadn't yet worked out whether that was a good or a bad thing. 'Peter, I can't go and live with her in Israel. I don't even know her.'

'What about your dad? Where is he?'

'Exactly. And who is he?'

The smell of roast coming from the kitchen made my mouth water as I stepped inside. Now I knew for sure that Mum had been hoarding our meat coupons.

'What are we having?' I asked.

'Canterbury lamb.' Mum had donned a wrap-around apron over her Sunday suit.

On the one hand, I was proud we could impress our guest. On the other, it made me cross to think of the many vegetarian Sundays when Mum might have been less frugal.

'We're having local lamb,' I told the Mutti, who was sitting in one of the upright armchairs by the tiled fireplace in the back room. She didn't look impressed, only fidgety. She was tapping the sides of her armchair.

Mum popped her head around the door. 'It's from Canterbury, New Zealand.' She gave a little laugh. 'Not British lamb, I'm afraid. Sorry.'

She could have got away with passing the lamb off as English but didn't do that. She was being the Mum I thought I knew, a stickler for the truth.

'I always thought Canterbury lamb was from here,' I said, so that everyone would know I hadn't meant to mislead.

The Mutti didn't seem to care either way. She only gazed out of the French windows, chewing her lip. At least she'd stopped tapping. I sat in the armchair opposite. We listened to Mum, busy in the kitchen. Without warning, the Mutti got to her feet and fled the room.

'Is everything alright, Mrs Levi?' I heard Mum say before the back door slammed.

Next thing, she was in the garden, hugging herself like it was cold, though it wasn't, and dragging on a cigarette. What a bundle of nerves she was. Was it her craving for cigarettes that made her that way, or the other way around?

Standing in the back room, watching her, with my arms folded across my chest, I deeply resented her self-indulgence. I was the one whose life had been turned on its head. Not her. If she was going to find the situation upsetting, she could have chosen to just leave us alone.

Mum was at the stove stirring the gravy when I came into the kitchen. She looked up and smiled at me. Leaning against the yellow Formica kitchen table, I said, as conversationally as I could, 'Would you ask her about my father?'

The wooden spoon jolted in her hand before continuing its circuit. Her head turned towards the kitchen door and something weird happened. It was like the ghost of Dad walked in, wearing the naval lieutenant's peaked cap and jacket from his picture in the back room, and the same smile. A chill went through me. At the same time, I was enraged that Mum had conditioned me to think this sainted war hero was my father.

'Yes, I'll do that.' She took down plates from the warmer above the cooker, seemingly unaware of the strong impulse I had to pick up the kitchen knife and plunge it into her back. 'Please go and tell Mutti it's ready.'

I stomped into the garden, glad to escape her. The Mutti was standing by the fence, smoking yet another cigarette. To my horror, answering puffs of smoke were rising on the other side. She was talking to Mr Price. I hoped she hadn't told him the whole story. If so, he'd be bound to tell Mrs Price, the megaphone of Lanfranc Close. Pretty soon, everyone would know I wasn't Mum's real daughter, but some foreigner.

'Dinner is ready,' I said. 'Please come.'

'Ach, good!'

I cringed at her German accent but, on the other side of the fence, Mr Price didn't seem at all fazed by it. He was feasting his eyes on her sparkling beauty.

As I drew level, he turned his attention to me. 'How's my best girl?'

Phew! He didn't know.

After we had all agreed how tasty the food was, the meal was one long, awkward silence. I wanted Mum to ask about my father, but she ignored my pleading looks.

Eventually, the Mutti said to Mum, 'It is very kind of you to invite me here. You are a good woman, for a goy.'

Mum looked a little taken aback. 'You're very welcome, Mrs Levi.'

'Please. It's Rochel.'

'What's a goy?' I asked.

Mutti turned to me. 'A goy is someone not a Jew. We cannot trust goyim.'

I thought her very rude to say that in front of Mum. But Mum didn't seem offended. In fact, she was nodding as if she agreed with her. 'We have a lot of ground to make up.'

The Mutti looked like she didn't understand.

'I mean,' Mum said, 'some non-Jews did terrible things to Jews during the war.'

'Yes.' The Mutti looked down at the table. I studied the muted greens and reds of the back-room wallpaper pattern – teapots and cruet sets – and sighed: clearly, she was one for dramatic pauses. Eventually, she said quietly, 'Lena, I have to tell you. We lost everyone. There's only me and you left.'

She seemed to assume I knew who *everyone* was. Her knuckles gripped the edge of the table, white as the tablecloth. Mum laid her hand over Mutti's: the white egg and the speckled egg. My two mothers, from two different worlds, were holding hands. Mum wore a wedding ring. Now I saw that the Mutti had none.

At last Mum asked the question I wanted her to. 'Was Marlene's biological father killed by the Nazis?'

'No!' She snatched her hand away. 'He was one of them!'

I immediately assumed she'd been forced. What a terrible kick-off for a mother–daughter relationship. It made me feel dirty. And surely it had to make her feel that way too. Small wonder she'd wanted to offload me. But it turned out to be a very different story.

'He was a handsome German boy; a Christian, not a Jew. He was very sweet with me and he made promises. I was fifteen. I believed them. We were in love, I thought. But Hitler was stirring up hate against the Jews and he listened to his friends. He joined the Hitler Youth.'

'What's that?'

'Boys playing soldiers,' she told me, 'using fighting words and learning to march up and down in uniform. Even so, I loved him, even when he began to hate me. He looked like a prince from a fairy tale. It began so lovely. But for him it was over. And you were...' She tapped her belly.

'Did you tell him?' Mum asked.

'I didn't tell no one, not him, not my own mother and father, not my sister Rifka, no one.' Her mouth was a rectangle of pain. 'My belly grew and time passed, and I remained still, like a rabbit in the car's headlights.'

Mum brought her a paper hankie. She blew her nose and continued, 'At first, after you were born, my family didn't want to know me no more. I had to make money for us to live as best I could. With time, they accepted us – you.' She looked at me. 'Everyone hated the Jews. We could all be hated together, I think.'

She took a deep breath. 'They're all dead, Lena. Your Oma and Opa and the Tante Rifka, your little cousin, Lottie

– taken away on trucks and trains and never seen or heard of again.'

Lottie – like my doll. I must have felt close to this cousin to call my doll after her. I had a vague recollection of dark plaits and height; a tall, thin girl. Nothing more. Something stirred, hazy pictures in my mind, like a movie I once saw. Oma and Opa were my grandparents. Tante Rifka had a handsome husband who threw me up in the air and caught me. I remembered climbing trees and playing make-believe with other kids. A deep sadness fell on me. I had family and they'd all perished.

I ignored Mum's touch on my arm. I had no space for her right now. In my mind's eye I was running in a vast garden with apple trees at the bottom of it, with my real family. They had loved me even though I was illegitimate, even though they may not even have known who my father was. I shuddered. No tragic Holocaust victim was he, and no hero either. How ironic that it should turn out I'd rather keep Dashing Dad than the real one. That made it like Mum had won. And she certainly didn't deserve that.

'So, I'm only half-Jewish?'

'You have a Jewish mother,' the Mutti said. 'That makes you Jew.'

'Judaism is passed down through the mother's line,' Mum said. How would she know that? She must have looked it up somewhere.

'What was his name?' I asked the Mutti.

'Whose name?'

'My father's, of course!'

Did I really want to know? Perhaps I was only pretending in order to get a reaction from Mum. But all she was doing right now was sending me a stern look for daring to shout at a grown-up.

'Peter.' The Mutti pronounced it Pay-ter.

My father had the same name as Peter next door!

'He called me Jew whore.' She was priceless. She had a gift for coming out with things you weren't supposed to say, and shocking Mum.

'He never knew he was the only one. Ach! When the war came he joined the army, of course.'

'Did he survive the war?'

'How should I know? I hope they sent him to the Russian Front to turn into an ice cube.'

So, I was still the girl with no father. If Mutti didn't know about him any more, I supposed I never would. Which was a hard thing to accept.

I was in the kitchen washing up the dishes, trying not to make a clatter so they'd forget I was there. I was listening in on their conversation.

Mum, who was sitting in her armchair knitting, was saying, 'You will allow Marlene to choose where she lives. Won't you?'

The Mutti was sitting across from her. 'Of course. She is a big girl, almost a woman.'

Mum didn't agree. She pointed out in her polite voice, 'Actually, she's still very young.'

Each saw what she wanted to. And they were both right. I was both.

'Of course, in the eyes of the law, she's a minor,' Mum said.

'I love her too much to make her come with me if she does not want to.' Mutti's words were beautiful. I smiled at the sudsy dinner plate I was washing.

'She may not want to.'

'Perhaps she will.'

Mum's voice sounded strained. 'Do you think you are a suitable mother for her?'

What a terrible thing to suggest. Strangely, the Mutti remained silent.

'I'm thinking of how she was when she arrived,' Mum went on. 'You know what I mean, I think.'

'I was hardly older than Lena is now. Everything would be different.' That sounded like a hedge. Not at all the reply I'd have expected from my feisty Mutti.

'Good,' Mum said, apparently satisfied.

And no more was said. Knitting needles clicked and I was left to wonder why the Mutti wouldn't be a 'suitable mother'.

Chapter Five

Even though exams were looming, my books remained largely unopened over the half-term holiday. That wasn't like me, but I had a mother to get to know.

Mum suggested we take her to Canterbury Cathedral, which is world-famous. On the way there, Mutti explained to Mum what I already knew: she didn't believe in Jesus. Jews didn't. I thought I must be the only one.

The million-dollar smile the Mutti sent the black-cassocked virger we met at the entrance reminded me of Hollywood actress Deanna Durbin and confirmed my suspicion that the Mutti was a flirt.

The virger, who was getting on a bit, looked first shocked, then terrified, then pleased.

'Good to see you. Good to see you,' he said. His eyes followed her hip-hugging skirt, as she swung inside, ahead of Mum and me.

The Mutti was twirling as we caught up with her. 'Ach, but it's beautiful!'

I looked around nervously. The heads of other visitors were turned in our direction. She wasn't just attracting attention to herself by behaving like a little girl. A lot of people in England didn't much go for German accents.

This visit was a bad idea. I was cross with Mum for suggesting it.

'Let's move on,' Mum said, and headed for the steps at the end of the nave.

'Why does everyone whisper?' the Mutti said in a loud voice as she trotted to catch up with us.

'This is a place of worship,' Mum whispered. It was clear from the Mutti's puzzled expression that the logic of this was passing her by.

We went down to the Martyrdom where, just after Christmas in the year 1170, Archbishop of Canterbury Thomas Becket was murdered by four knights sent by King Henry II, who burst in on him. This had been a topic at school and I was able to explain the murder in gruesome detail, despite the wide eyes Mum was making at me to stop. I pointed out the red stain on the floor tiles, though my teacher was sure this was not Thomas' blood.

As we wandered from the cloister towards what was once an ornate water tower for the monks, we ran into the virger again. He told Mutti how God had spared the cathedral during the bombardment of 1942, 'thanks to the bravery of the firemen, who stood on the roof, kicking off incendiary bombs as they fell'. However, a big bomb had dropped on the library, which we could see from the pile of rubble right in front of us. 'It would have been a terrible blow to morale if the cathedral had been destroyed.'

Mum sighed. 'People have flooded here over the centuries, hoping for a blessing.'

'A blessing from God,' the virger said. 'A lot of who we are as a nation is tied up in this cathedral.'

Much to all our surprise, Mutti suddenly burst out, '*Quatsch*!'

'Pardon?' Mum said.

The virger looked particularly put out.

Mutti waved her arms. 'Such rubbish about firemen saving an old building. You value things and not people here. People you let die.'

'Well, I must be running along.' The virger shuffled away.

'I know of lots of times the war brought out the very best in people,' I said.

Mum looked angry. 'It's true we had looters and black-market sharks. But there were also countless sacrificial acts of bravery.'

Mutti's eyes took on a hard brilliance. 'Your war was not my war.'

Something about all the hurt she so obviously held inside made me reach for her hand.

Mum winced.

She didn't come out with us again. Mutti and I went on the bus to Margate without her and had a super time. Mutti was chummy, like a big sister. She was fearless. Her clothing, her opinions and her bluntness could be troubling or like juicy dates at Christmas. Mum, by comparison, seemed limp and wishy-washy.

We rode the Scenic Railway at Dreamland and the Octopus, the Ghost Train, and the Magic Carpet ride. We swam in the Lido. We sat on the sand eating fish and chips wrapped in newspaper and we ate candyfloss as we watched a Punch and Judy show.

Mutti got right into the plot. 'That Punch is a monster. He threw the baby away. And hit his wife.' She was outraged. 'She had a Jewish name – Judy. Was she Jewish?'

I had no idea. That was one thing about her: she was looking for prejudice all the time. It was always at the forefront of her mind. Perhaps she saw my father in Punch. Though she never said he hit her, he had gone the route of violence. It was strange to think that if he didn't die in the war, he would be somewhere out there. It was hard to hate him for the Nazi he was when every time I tried to picture him, an image of Peter next door popped into my head.

We returned from Margate to find Mum sitting in her armchair in the back room. She was spending a lot of time there, staring out of the French windows. She didn't have a whole lot to say for herself these days. She didn't care enough to fight for me and that was OK by me. I didn't care either.

Babs was among the crowd of passengers getting off the bus that squealed to a halt beside me as I walked to school dressed in my summer uniform – panama, blazer and dress – with my heavy satchel on my back. She waved her arms and called to me.

'Hi, Daddy-O,' I replied. I was pleased to see my best chum after a whole week apart.

'I jumped off a stop early when I saw you,' she said.

That was nice of her.

We set off together, past historic High Street buildings blackened by traffic, like the ornate Victorian Beaney library, one of my favourite haunts. This end of town had escaped the bombs. The pavement, busy with school children and people off to work, wasn't wide enough for us to walk side by side. I had to keep turning back to talk to her. 'How was the holiday?'

'Butlin's was just the bee's knees.' She had to shout above the traffic so I could hear. 'They have a huge swimming pool, a coffee bar and a bar. It's so keen. There are shows every night and they screen the latest films.'

'You're wearing eye shadow.' It was light blue. She had shocking pink nails and her mane of platinum hair was a mass of waves at the back. She was going to be in a heap of trouble at school again.

'A girl has to keep up appearances, especially when she's Miss Butlin's.' Babs smirked.

'What's that?'

We turned off by Boots the Chemist, which was in a really old building from Tudor times, or maybe even earlier. Now we could walk two abreast.

'I won the beauty contest. I got a voucher to spend at the shop. I bought scent.' I could smell it. Flowery. That was another school rule she was breaking.

'Congratulations.'

Babs was pretty; overdone, but pretty. I could just see her, parading up and down the length of the pool in her swimming costume.

'Really, I couldn't have gone in for something like that.'

'I didn't have much choice.' She laughed. 'The Redcoats pulled me out of my seat.'

'Who?' I thought Redcoats were English soldiers from olden times, with muskets.

'They're the entertainment staff.'

'How awful to be forced into it.' I suspected she hadn't been that unwilling. 'The only beauty contest where I've ever won a prize was playing Monopoly.'

She looked puzzled. 'What?'

'You know, when you get to take a card from the Community Chest and it tells you you've won second prize in a beauty contest.'

We both laughed.

She switched to her pitying face. 'It must have been soooooo boring for you, stuck at home.'

If only she knew.

'Not at all,' I said.

'What did you do with yourself?'

As I was thinking how to answer this, she leaned in confidentially. 'I met a boy. He's sixteen.'

'A boyfriend, Babs?'

She grinned. 'Yes.'

I was impressed. 'Did he take you out?'

She giggled. 'To the sand dunes at the back of the beach.' It sounded romantic. 'He was a real dish. All the girls were after him, but he picked me because I was Miss Butlin's.' A few yards further on she added, 'He told me he loved me.'

I couldn't imagine a boy saying he loved me. 'Maybe you'll marry him.'

'Daddy wouldn't approve. He's a cosh boy.'

'What's a cosh boy?'

'Oh, Marlene, what bush have you been hiding under? Cosh boys have the kiss curls on top, and sideburns. They wear drainpipe trousers.'

'Oh, those boys.' There were a few around here. Loud and coarse, they roved around in packs and made me glad I went to an all-girls school. 'I thought you wanted someone like your dad, a war hero?'

She tugged down her shirt collar to show me a mottled blue bruise on her neck. It looked sore. 'Ooh, you poor thing. How did you get that?'

'It's a love bite!'

'He bit you? Was he a vampire?'

She snorted. 'You're just jealous.'

'No, I'm not.' I was, but not how she thought. I was jealous of the smug little fortress of family life she didn't value enough to listen to her father's wishes.

'Will you even see him again?' I asked, not a little nastily.

For once, Babs looked unsure. 'I gave him my address. He said he'd write. But he lives in Birmingham.' That was hours and hours away.

'Does he have a name?'

'John.'

'John from Birmingham.'

'He had an accent.' She laughed and imitated it. 'He squeezed his words out through his nose like this.'

Though I laughed along with her, I was sad for Babs, whose heart would surely be broken.

That seemed to be the way of things for us females. Mum's heart was broken when Dad died. I was sure Mutti's must have been too, when her Peter turned against her. This set me wondering about our class teacher, Miss MacGrotty. She was part of a whole generation of women condemned to pine throughout their lives for the 10 million who never returned from the First World War. And poor Mrs Price, married to Peter's letch of a dad. Possibly, she felt just as alone. Probably, Peter was her only comfort. If he were my boyfriend, I might wind up as hurt as everyone else. It was far better for a girl to be an adventurous spirit – a 'derring-do' explorer of the world – than to ache for love.

'You're looking fierce, Marlene,' Babs said. 'Penny for your thoughts?'

As she said this, the bell above the door of the general store we were passing tinkled and Peter came through it, munching on his entire sweetie ration for the month. So absorbed was he in his chocolate that he came down the step and practically walked into the two of us. We crab-stepped around on the pavement for a while. Peter and I were laughing. Babs looked bewildered.

When the three of us stopped dancing the quadrille, I said, 'Morning.'

'How are you?' He looked like he'd been worrying about me and really wanted to know. I hadn't seen him the whole week, which was different from how the holidays usually went.

I could feel my cheeks flushing scarlet. I was embarrassed about pretty much everything: the distress I'd shared with him about Mutti; the intensity of his gaze; the presence of my friend, standing beside me done up like a painted doll; and the fact that she could probably read me like a book.

'Very well, thank you.'

'Hello,' Babs said. 'I'm Babs.' Now I felt guilty for not introducing her.

'Peter.'

What happened next I would play over and over to myself in slow motion in the days and months that followed. With a little shimmy of the shoulders and a secretive half-smile, she sent him a killer up-and-under look. Peter looked momentarily stunned, then grinned broadly at her, looking more like a sheepdog than it should be possible for any human to look.

Hatred for them both flashed through me.

Chapter Six

As I came up the stairs after school that afternoon, Mutti was standing in her bedroom doorway, wearing her slacks, red top and red lips. Her hair hung loose about her shoulders. She smiled, which perked me up. I'd walked home alone, not wanting to talk to anyone.

'Tell me about you, Lena, so-grown-up-now. Who have you become?'

What a question! I laughed. But her brown eyes were studying me, clearly expecting an answer.

'I'm, well, I'm...' The tears that welled took me by surprise. Little more than a week ago I might have reeled off my name, age and where I lived. Now I didn't know the person I'd started out as. So how could I say anything about who she'd become?

'Come, talk,' Mutti said.

She stepped back to allow me into the room. Actually, it was my room. I'd moved into the spare room when she first arrived. This room was a lot bigger and gave on to the back of the house.

It had been a boy's room, with steam trains on the walls, when we moved in. Mum decorated it with a wallpaper we picked out together: sprigs of pink rosebuds with mint-green leaves on a white background. The war was over, and we were able to leave behind the rubbery blackout blinds we'd covered our windows with in Wales. The curtains we chose were aqua with a white fleck. The eiderdown was cherry-and-green paisley. It was a lovely room, though now it smelled of Mutti, instead of me.

I sat on the bed, which was really my bed, with my back against the wooden headboard. She sat at the foot, like a doctor in a hospital. 'I want to tell you my story.'

I gaped at her. Squirmy as I felt about it, I was expecting the conversation to be about me, especially as, until now, she hadn't asked me one single thing about myself. On second thoughts, though, I wasn't sorry to be with her. There was a lot I still wanted to know.

Her mouth twisted this way and that. I could see she was wondering how to begin. 'It was a big, shameful thing for your grandparents to have a pregnant daughter.'

That was understandable. Nice girls didn't. Mutti had. Did that make her bad? Maybe just very foolish, I decided.

'My school sent me away.'

'They expelled you? How terrible!'

'That was how my parents found out. I did not find the courage to tell them myself.' She cleared her throat. 'They looked at me like they hated me. They didn't want anyone from *shul* – from the synagogue – to know. That was the most important to them. We weren't a strict Jewish family, but we were known.' She broke off and looked towards the heavy grey clouds outside. 'It was a bad time.'

For a moment everything outside the window seemed to be holding its breath. Then the leaves fluttered and a pitter-patter of rain began. I'd got home just in time.

'Naturally, they wanted to know who the father was...'

'*My* father?'

'Yes.'

'But I sat on the dining table swinging my legs like I didn't care and wouldn't tell them.'

It was strange to think that I was there too – in her belly, unaware – with no say in any of it. Her dirty secret was me.

'Since they couldn't marry me off to a father without a name, they sent me out of their sight. They sent me to live with a German woman who lived on the other side of Bremen.'

'A German woman?' I wondered what she meant by that. 'Wasn't everyone German? Weren't you?'

'That's what we called non-Jews.'

'I see.'

This must have meant they saw their Jewishness as their race, not just their religion. Peter's assertion that the Jews needed a homeland suddenly fell into place.

'The arrangement was that I looked after the house instead of paying rent. But I was really a servant. I had no money, apart from small amounts my mother would give me from time to time. It was a big change from being their darling daughter.'

I knew exactly how that felt since it was turning out that Mum didn't care to keep me either.

'I should not speak bad of the dead.' Mutti sighed. 'My parents did the best they were able.'

Rain was drumming on the shed roof. There was a rumble of distant thunder. She stared out at the weather. 'Do you remember our little room in the roof?'

Her question startled me. I hadn't thought about the German woman's place being my home too. I shook my head, remembering nothing.

'We lived there three years, Lena.' Her tone was reproachful. 'You were born in that room.'

A black void. 'I don't remember.'

'It was so cold up there and the midwife who came to deliver you was also like ice – because you had spoiled her Christmas and because you had no father.' Her liquid eyes, filled with sadness, met mine. Her tone, when she continued, was bitter. 'And because I was Jew. It wasn't always so in Germany. Hitler had already spread his poison.' A smile broke through. I was grateful for the change of atmosphere it brought. 'But you were a beautiful baby, Lena. Perfect. I named you Marlene, after Marlene Dietrich.' She said it Mar-lay-na Deet-rick.

'I'm nothing like her.' Marlene Dietrich was an ageing German actress with platinum blonde hair and a husky voice.

Why did I have to be this woman's child? It would have been so good if she could have been my sister.

'At first, my landlady had many strict rules regarding you. But she liked you and got softer.'

'Who was she?'

'No one. Her name was Frau Schumacher.'

'What about my grandparents? Didn't they relent?' I thought they must have, since I kind of felt like I remembered – or sensed that there had been – family time.

'We didn't go to Oma and Opa's house, never. They never stopped being ashamed. But we took the tram out to the end of the line, to the house of Rifka and her family, and we saw them there. You liked the tram.'

I tried to remember rattling along in a tram and liking it, but nothing came. However, something sparked for me when she said, 'I found work singing and dancing in a beer cellar. It paid for clothing and tram tickets.'

I threw up my hands. 'I used to go with you!'

She shook her head. 'No. Frau Schumacher looked after you.' She frowned before continuing hesitantly, 'Maybe you did, sometimes. Frau Schumacher could be…' Mutti pursed her lips.

'Pouty?' I suggested.

'She did it when she felt like it.'

'I wet my knickers at the beer cellar one time.'

Her eyes widened. '*Schatzi,* you remember that?'

Something stirred in my belly as she said *schatzi.* I thought she must have used that term of endearment with me when I was small, though I had no recollection of it.

Yet this fragile half-memory of mine felt oddly dark.

She leaned forward, speaking earnestly. 'I never wanted to hurt you.'

I didn't know whether she meant the subject in hand, or our whole relationship. It felt safer to assume she meant the former. 'I suppose you had to finish your act. You couldn't very well break off and deal with me.'

A strange smile, almost a smirk, crossed her face. She looked like she'd got away with something. It was very puzzling.

'Tea is ready!' Mum called from the bottom of the stairs. For a short while now, there had been clattering in the kitchen – cymbals to accompany the drum rolls of thunder unleashed by the heavens.

I stayed where I was, sitting on the bed, summoning up my courage until I was able to say, 'I want to know how I got here.'

The rain was teeming now. It was splashing on the windowsill. Mutti got up to shut the window. 'After supper.'

'No, now.'

She turned back towards me, framed by the black sky behind her. 'Things were getting harder and harder for the Jews. The Germans hated us.' Her flat tone and lack of emotion made her words chilling. 'We all talked about leaving. Your Oma didn't believe what was happening. "All my friends are in Bremen," she said. "What evil will they do to us? We belong here."' She sneered. 'Ha! We others wanted to try to get to Israel, but that was not for my mother... "It will be too warm for me there," she said.'

Her mouth became a hard line and she looked away, at tears running down the window. I wanted to do something to ease her pain but didn't know how. So, I did nothing, which made me feel useless and awkward.

She sounded matter-of-fact when she spoke again. 'It grew clear things weren't going to get better. Then came *Kristallnacht,* the Night of Broken Glass. Everyone talks about the damage to shops, but it wasn't just Jewish businesses that were smashed that night.' She coughed and cleared her throat. 'That night, young people – boys from the neighbourhood, like my Peter – went into houses. They shot Jews in their beds, or took them outside and murdered them.' She shook her head as if she still couldn't fathom the reason for it. 'The whole of Germany was against us.'

'Did you hear me?' Mum called up from downstairs. 'It's ready.'

I opened my mouth to shout at her to leave us alone, but my throat was dry as dust and I couldn't speak.

'We are coming,' Mutti answered. A flash of sheet lightning turned the sky bluey-white, closely followed by a loud crash of thunder. We both jumped.

'We should go down,' she said. The sound rumbled around the sky, on and on. Neither of us moved.

'Two months later, in January of 1939, Rifka said she'd heard England was taking Jewish children. I went to my old rabbi. It was hard to make myself go. I had the feeling I was betraying my parents by telling my secret. And I thought he also would look down on me.' She mimed how hard it was by 'making' herself go to the bedroom door. 'He was astounded that I had a child, but he was kind. He contacted the Care of Children people from England and arranged everything. Your ship left from Bremen the following June. It was a relief.' Mutti chewed her lip. 'Your cousin Lottie was supposed to go with you, to save herself and take care of you. At the last minute she didn't want to go. And Rifka told her, "Alright, stay."'

Heat surged through me. Lottie hadn't wanted to go. So, she stayed. But Mutti had been eager to get rid of me!

Mutti saw my fierce face and became businesslike. 'By September, three months later, Germany and Britain were at war and the borders closed. Come.'

She went out. I heard her go into the bathroom. I breathed deeply and reminded myself that Lottie was dead and I wasn't. So, who was the good mother? The trees had worked themselves into a frenzy. They were shaking their leafy branches at me as I got to my feet.

I was thinking about being there, in Germany, on that murderous night and not being aware of anything that had happened, any more than I had been aware of Mutti's family circumstances. I had been put on a ship and couldn't remember that either. It was like I had amnesia or something.

I dragged myself down the stairs. My feelings towards Mutti ebbed and flowed like the tide. One minute I'd feel close and the next distant; one minute I'd like her and the next not. Or I'd feel like covering my ears and going la-la-la because I didn't want to hear what she had to tell me. I hated hardly remembering anything of this story that was supposed to be mine. Where were the memories I should have had? Where had they gone? And why?

Mum and I sat at the table in the back room, waiting for her. After a few minutes with no sign of her, Mum put her palms together and said grace. I chewed on my half-cold cheese on toast mechanically as the clock on the mantelpiece ticked away the seconds. My eyes fell on the big basket of neatly ironed linen on the couch. Monday was washing day. The world could be caving in and Mum would make sure I had a freshly laundered shirt for school. That was Mum. Would *she* have put me on a boat all alone and sent me away?

I was cross Mutti hadn't come down. Questions were giving rise to questions. I needed to interrogate her.

Eventually, Mum spoke, picking her words like stepping stones. 'When you make your choice, Marlene, it doesn't have to be forever. You can change your mind later, either way.'

She seemed to expect a response, so I nodded. 'I know.'

Mutti finally came down the stairs as I was getting my last mouthful down.

'So!' She clapped her hands. 'The rain is stopping.'

Mum and I turned to the window. If you were willing to really stretch a point, you could allow that it was easing off, maybe a very little bit.

'I suppose,' I said.

She lifted her knife and fork, poised to tuck in with gusto. But it was all show. There were streaks of mascara around her eyes.

Chapter Seven

The weather cleared up after tea. Mum sent Mutti and me off for a walk while she washed up. We got wet ankles crossing school playing fields to the woods where all the greens were vibrant and everything smelled fresh.

Mutti jabbered about the importance of the water level in the Sea of Galilee and how it was looking this year – not very encouraging, according to her. Clearly, it was a very different country from England.

I realised she wasn't going to volunteer any of the information I needed. So, I asked her the question that was driving me crazy. It came out like an accusation. 'When the war was over, why didn't you come and get me?'

She didn't seem to notice. 'So much was lost, I… What can I say?' She chewed on her lip. 'It was like I wasn't me any more. And you, it was like you were a character in a dream I once had on a summer's afternoon in the garden at Rifka's house – food and laughter, a day so perfect it perhaps never happened.'

'But I am real, Mutti!' For some stupid reason, *The Merchant of Venice*, which we had been studying this term, popped into my head. 'If you cut me, do I not bleed?' I could see from her blank expression she had no idea what I was saying.

'"If you prick us, do we not bleed?"' I said, verbatim this time, for we had learned the passage by heart. '"If you tickle us, do we not laugh? If you poison us, do we not die? And if you wrong us, shall we not revenge?"'

'I never cut you, Lena!'

'It's Shakespeare. Shylock the Jew's speech.'

'Ach, I thought you were angry with *me*.'

I was. Furious. 'Go on.'

'As my strength returned, I thought about you more and more. All the time.'

The path we were following narrowed. She walked behind me. Suddenly, the slanting sun burst through the leaves of the beech trees we were passing, dappling the woodland floor with gold. It also cast its glow on a broad patch of chlorophyll-coloured ferns off to our left, turning it into an enticing fairyland. I waited for her to say more, but she was silent. There was only the creaking and cracking of damp trees all around us.

'You left me here.'

'Was that so bad?'

'That's not the point.' How could it be when I didn't know I was in the wrong place?

'Dov, the kibbutz leader, helped me search for you. It wasn't easy. You weren't at the address in Wales they had. In the end they found you here, in Canterbury. The kibbutz paid for my trip.'

I wheeled around to face her. 'It's 1950. The war ended *five years ago*! Where were you? Come to that, where were you in the war? How did you survive?' She winced as if my questions were blows.

'I just didn't go out any more, not to work, or to shops, or anywhere. They would make me wear a yellow badge with *Jude* on it. They would sneer at me, spit on me, or put me on a truck and take me away.' She sighed. 'There was no more family for me. I did not even dare peek through the curtains. I was dependent on Frau Schumacher. She told the shopkeepers and neighbours I'd run away or something, she didn't know. She told them I wasn't there when she came back one day. Maybe I'd been taken like the other dirty Jews.

'The truth was that I was up in my little room, freezing in winter, sweating in summer. I hid in the wardrobe every time anyone came, which was seldom. She was a lonely old woman.'

'So, she was kind?' That hadn't been the impression I'd got of her before.

Mutti snorted. 'I began as her servant. Now I was her slave.'

'What do you mean?'

'What I say.'

When it became plain she wasn't going to add to that, we continued along the path to a clearing where we watched the sun playing hide-and-seek between scudding clouds, trying to make us believe the storm had never been.

My feelings were scudding like those clouds. Mutti had had a hard time of it, for sure. Yet, in some ways, hers was a happy story. She'd escaped the gas chambers and, somehow, made it to Israel. I tried to feel compassion for her, but I couldn't. The hurt of abandon was too raw.

'You never wrote. Why didn't you write?'

She waved away my complaint like a bothersome fly. 'Ach! I don't write. I do.'

My eyes teared up, which made me angry with myself. I didn't want her to see she had the power to make me cry.

She leaned in towards me and spoke in a low voice. 'You think I'm tough, but I wasn't always so. Once, I was more like you. I did what I was told. It was easier than thinking about what was lost.'

I turned away and walked on. She was wrong about me. I was tough as old boots, a girl of action. I'd show her. Somehow. She didn't know me.

We arrived home to the rhythm of big band music coming from the wireless set on top of Mum's sewing machine cabinet in the back room. She turned the volume down and made a pot of tea. We sat around the back-room fireplace drinking it while Mum knitted.

'How did you get to Israel after the war?' she asked Mutti, knitting needles clicking. She was on the second sleeve of a new navy school cardigan for me.

'Well, Bremen was an ugly place after the war. A Jew would be *meshugenah* to stay there.'

Memories stirred at that strange, yet oddly familiar, word. Mutti, and perhaps the whole family, loved to use it when they called someone crazy.

Mutti looked bitter. 'Strangers lived in Rifka's house now and in the house of my parents also. You could still feel the hatred in the sideways looks in the street, even though it wasn't me who had caused their pain, their shame in losing.'

She sipped her tea, which she took without milk and with heaps of sugar. Mum and I took milk in our tea, of course, and had weaned ourselves off sugar, which was still rationed.

'I had to live in a camp for displaced persons. I spoke to someone who knew someone from the Jewish Agency. They helped me get to Israel, even though it was illegal. It was a hard journey, to go unseen through Austria and into Italy, to go on a ship in the black night. All the time, I thought of my mother, who was lost – I didn't know how – and her silly words about Israel being too hot. When I finally arrived, the English took me off the boat and put me in a detention camp.'

'What?' A big gulp of hot tea burned the inside of my mouth. My cup wobbled as I thumped it back on its saucer. I was horrified that my own people could be so heartless. 'How come?'

Mum supplied the answer. 'Israel was under a British Mandate until 1948.'

'What's that?'

'We were in charge of the country.'

'So, why wouldn't we let the Jews live normally?'

'Don't raise your voice, Marlene. *I* didn't incarcerate your mother.'

How dare she say *your mother* like she was disowning me? '*I* wasn't raising my voice!' I paused for breath and controlled my tone. 'I don't understand how we could put them in camps, like the Germans.'

Mutti's laughter was hollow. 'No one wanted us, not anywhere, not even in Israel. The British took some to Cyprus, others to places in the Indian Ocean. Some were even sent back to the displaced persons camps in Germany. I was lucky, I suppose, because I remained in Israel, even though I was a prisoner: I was sent to Atlit, near Haifa.'

I glowered, ashamed my own country had done that.

'Ach! No need to look sad. It wasn't so bad. There was food and soap. They arranged things for us to do, because we could not go out. Above all there was hope – as soon as it was agreed we would get our own nation.' She certainly liked the word *hope.*

She turned to Mum. 'How did you get to Canterbury after the war?'

Something silky about the way she asked this put Mum on the defensive. 'We weren't on the run or anything. We weren't trying to hide from you.'

'No?'

'No.' She spoke to me as if Mutti wasn't there. 'We couldn't manage the farm without Dad, not long-term. Anyway, it wasn't ours. It belonged to Grandpa – Daddy's dad – who was too old to run it. He asked us to move out after Uncle Owen was demobbed – that was in 1944 after he caught typhoid. He and his family moved in with us and I stayed on to help out for a while. We finally left in '46.'

Uncle Owen was Dad's younger brother. We haven't seen him or any of Dad's family since.

'Dad,' Mutti repeated, with emphasis. *'Grandpa, Uncle Owen.'*

She was right, I supposed. None of these people were really my relatives. Not even Mum. A thought that left me teetering on a cliff edge.

Mum put her knitting into one hand to drink her tea. She turned to Mutti. 'My husband left me enough to give us the start here we needed.'

'And you told no one.'

'There was nothing secret about it. This was where I grew up.'

The silence that followed was filled with hostility. I hurried to change the subject. 'Is Israel like England?'

Mutti looked at me like I was doolally. 'Not at all.'

I didn't think the suggestion so far-fetched. I'd read a novel about Kenya, which was a colony rather than a mandate. Kenya had its own geography and climate but British ways.

'What is it like? I mean, to live there.'

It was gratifying to see Mum's knitting wobble in her hand as she glanced my way.

Mutti's eyes took on a gleam. 'Madness, a wonderful madness, alive with colour and light.'

'Golly!' I enthused, watching Mum. But her eyes remained fixed on her teacup this time.

Mutti looked pleased with my reaction. 'Now I live on Kibbutz Eshkadosh. That also is a bit like a camp.' She laughed. 'Only the barbed wire is to keep the bad people *out*.'

Exams were starting the next day. Normally, I enjoyed getting my teeth into algebra practice exercises. (Weird? Yeah, that's me.) Yet I was chewing on the end of my pencil and staring out of the window at a crop of raindrops still glistening on the weeping willow's tendrils. How could I revise for anything when everything inside was swirling?

The world Mum had constructed around me, the life I had felt safe in, was a sham and I hated her with a passion for that. The fact that she didn't seem to care whether I stayed or left made me hate her all the more.

Mutti was just as bad and totally untrustworthy. She hadn't even bothered to try to find me sooner. I wished with all my heart I could just lift the dust sheets off my past to resurrect our relationship, but even if I scrunched up my eyes and concentrated hard, I still couldn't remember anything, beyond blows raining on my head.

What?

With a jolt I saw the theatre curtain go down to hoots and applause. It was the Night of the Wee. Mutti towered above me in her top hat and black stockings, hands on hips, her legs silhouetted against the stage lights splaying out from under the curtain behind her.

I cowered, knowing what would come next, and dreading it. I remembered the jarring of my teeth as slaps rained on my face, shoulders and arms. My hands were raised to shield myself. I was trying with all my might not to cry out. If I did, it would be worse. Not then, maybe, but later.

Punches hit my head, my body, followed by more stinging slaps. I fell to the floor.

She only stopped when the stagehand in the brown overall cried, 'Enough!'

And the very next day, or so it seemed, she packed a little suitcase for me and rode with me on the tram to the port in silence – a long, long journey that felt as if it would never end. She tied on a brown, craft label like I was a parcel and left me with hundreds of other bad children whose fate, like mine, was to be sent away.

Up the gangplank we shuffled, onto the high vessel. Docked alongside and all around were great, grey warships with huge guns on their decks. Men in dark uniforms swarmed everywhere. In my mind we were their prisoners.

The other children were bigger than me. They chattered away as if they knew one another. I realised now that they probably didn't. Most likely they were alone and scared, like me. The tremors going through me now, setting my teeth chattering as I sat on the couch with my algebra book open in my lap, were an echo of the terror then. I was afraid I'd wet myself again and be punished. I was afraid of the men in uniform, afraid of the towering ship.

I watched the memory in disbelief. It was like being in a nightmare and knowing it, but unable to control how events unfolded. Because they were real. I was all alone with only One–Eyed Lottie tucked under my arm for comfort.

In the hanger, when we had been told to say our goodbyes, I'd reached, trembling, for the cotton wool of safety. 'I'm sorry, Mutti.'

Like a thousand other mothers there, she bent to kiss me. 'Be a good girl.'

'Please forgive me!' I begged. 'Please, Mutti! I didn't mean it. Take me home.'

Her high heels clicked like knitting needles as she walked away.

I exploded into Mutti's bedroom. 'Why did you come?'

Sitting on my bed, she looked up in surprise from painting her nails.

'You don't love me! You never loved me! What are you doing here? You're only here to make trouble.'

Her tone was abrupt. 'Come and sit down and we will talk calmly.'

I remained clinging to the door. 'You used to beat me!'

She waved it away like it was nothing. 'Ach! I am sorry for that.'

I don't know what I expected – remorse, perhaps; or, at the very least, a show of shame. Certainly not her what-can-you-do shrug that only fanned my flames. 'How could you?'

She patted the bed. 'Sit down.'

'No!'

'Sit down, I say.'

'Or else?'

Mum appeared behind me, flustered. 'What's all this shouting, Marlene?'

I was blocking the doorway. The only way to let her into the room was to move into it, nearer to Mutti, but I kept my distance and pointed my finger. 'She used to beat me!'

'Ah,' Mum said, like she knew.

'I want her to sit down,' Mutti told Mum. 'I need to tell her things. You too.'

Mum went and sat on the bed at Mutti's feet, siding with her. They both looked my way.

Eventually, I gave ground and sat cross-legged on the floor, a yard away from the foot of the bed, my shoulders tight with hostility. My insides didn't match my face. They were jelly. I couldn't take very much more of this.

Mutti carefully twisted the cap back on her nail varnish. Her nails were now cherry red like her sweater. 'I wasn't going to tell. But I must.' She placed the bottle on the bedside table. 'No one wants to talk about certain things. There is shame in them, which is strange because we did nothing. But sometimes they must be spoken.'

She hadn't done nothing. She had hit me. How many times had it happened? Often? I expected to hear excuses and justifications. Nothing could have prepared me for what followed.

She heaved a heavy sigh. 'In 1944, I was arrested by the Gestapo.'

'But you said you spent the war hiding at your landlady's!'

It looked as if more lies were about to come out. There was no picking a path through them, it seemed. You had to wait for people to own up, or just live as though no one could be counted on. My life had become the kind of western where, when you see a low branch, you just know it will drag the cowboy from his horse into quicksand.

Mutti said, 'One day in October, Frau Schumacher went out for groceries and didn't come back. A few days later, a man and a woman came. They had keys. They went all over the house, looking to see what she had. And they found me hiding in the wardrobe.'

It was Mum's turn to sigh. 'Oh dear.'

'They were her son and daughter-in-law.' Mutti spoke in a hoarse monotone. 'They had never once visited her in all the years I was there. I made as if I was a regular German, renting. If that was so, why was I in the wardrobe? "In this time, everybody hides from strangers,"

I told them. "You were going through the house, searching. I thought you were burglars." They said Frau Schumacher had a heart attack in the street and was in the hospital. I said I would visit her. They left.' Her face grew tight. 'I thought it was in order, that they believed me. But the next morning before dawn, a Gestapo truck came. They arrested me. It was all shouting and shoving and insults. They took me in a truck to the railway station, where I waited and waited. In the end, a train came. It was no passenger train. We were put on a cattle truck.'

'Who was "we"?' I sniped. 'I thought you were alone?'

'All the other Jews they had caught.'

'Hadn't they already taken everyone by 1944?'

'They were still finding French Jews and Dutch Jews and Belgian Jews in hiding. There were Italians, Hungarians, Greeks, Russians, Romanians, even a few from Germany, like me. No one was an exception.'

She swung her feet around to the floor and went to the window. Leaning on the sill, she stared out. I could see pinpricks of night gathering and the birds were singing goodnight to one another. It was a pretty evening, a normal evening, which seemed so strange.

'Believe me,' she said, 'we were many. We travelled like the cattle, standing. Though the train was full, more Jews were added at every stop. It lasted for hours. Maybe it was days. I don't know any more. Three died. One was a child, a little girl with all her life in front of her. We pushed the bodies into a corner.'

I was still not believing her. 'What if you wanted the lavatory?'

'We made a corner for that too.'

I pulled a face. 'It must have got stinky.'

'Hush, Marlene,' Mum said.

Mutti turned to face us. 'Even though the place we came to was cold and unwelcoming, just a long platform with flat fields around it and the wind carrying flakes of early snow, it was *so* good to get off that train, good to be able to breathe the air again. As the carriages emptied, the platform filled. We were so many people. We hugged ourselves against the biting weather as the selection began.' She wrapped her arms around her chest and held herself tight, as if to show us. 'Families were broken up. There was crying and begging.'

My arms were also folded across my chest, but in annoyance. I failed to understand how any of what Mutti was telling us justified what she did to me, all of which took place *before*. It was the web of deceit that was my own history I wanted to hear about, which was far worse than her story.

'The soldiers shouted at us,' Mutti said. 'They hit the old men and butted the children with their rifles.'

'Did that upset you?' I was being sarcastic. No doubt she was as unmoved by these strangers as she had been tough with me at the dockside. And I still wasn't convinced she was telling the truth.

'I was exhausted. My will was to put one foot in front of the other and stand up straight and show no weakness. Everything for me depended on going the opposite side from the old men and the children.'

'And you did,' Mum said.

Mutti turned to her. 'I was strong. They put me to work.'

'What kind of work?' I said.

She shrugged. 'I don't know, pointless work, sorting things.'

The look on her face said, 'Don't ask more.' I rolled my eyes, but she didn't notice. She was away with her thoughts. Or maybe she was making a performance of it, which I thought more likely. She clearly had enticed poor, gullible Mum into her web.

All at once, she smirked. Her hips began to sway. 'The SS officers wanted me to sing and dance for them...' Her lips moved to music inside her head.

Mum looked shocked. I knew what she was thinking. I realised that soirées like she was remembering might include a whole lot more than singing and dancing.

'You were not there. So, you should not judge,' she said, seeing my face. 'It got me extra food rations. I survived.' A memory seemed to hit her. 'I found out Rifka and Lottie had been gassed. But I never knew what happened to your Oma and Opa or to anyone from the synagogue. When I went back to Bremen after the war, not one Jew was there. No one came back. Ha! Even Frau Schumacher had died.'

'Hang on,' I said. 'You didn't finish telling us about the concentration camp.'

'It's not a story to entertain, Marlene,' Mum said.

'I know!'

'It's OK,' Mutti turned to me. 'Life was cheap in the camps, Lena. Every day people were killed. After a gassing, they'd open the doors and bodies would tumble out like potatoes. Officers shot people for fun.' How could she talk about all of this so matter-of-factly? 'Others dropped where they worked or didn't wake up in the morning. We all knew that sooner or later, it would be our turn. And that didn't seem important.'

'So how *did* you make it through?' I couldn't keep the scepticism from my voice.

'I was lucky to be captured late. I was also lucky to get a fever so bad I couldn't join the forced marches to other death camps. Thousands set out and were never seen again. You see, every day we could hear the guns getting closer. The guards knew – and we knew – that the Allies were coming. We thought the guards would murder us all and try to escape.'

'The Allies?'

'Yes, Marlene, our side,' Mum said, joining Mutti at the window. 'The British and Americans and everyone fighting the Germans.'

Mutti looked at Mum. 'In the end, the guards just ran off. It was the Red Army that came, the Russians. They were silent when they saw us. And no wonder. We were like stick people. When we showed them how it was, all of it, the soldiers wept.'

Mum laid a hand on her shoulder. Now they were going to be friends, with me looking on, an owlish outsider, refusing to be hoodwinked.

'One young man gave me and my friend chocolate. It was too rich. I was sick. My friend died after eating it. We'd had nothing but watery soup for weeks.' Her eyes filled with tears. 'For her it was over.'

Eventually, Mum returned to sit on the bed again. She patted down her skirt, signalling a return to decorum, though she looked upset. Mutti wiped her eyes and blew her nose.

'Bedtime.' I scrambled to my feet. 'I have exams tomorrow. Night.' Their looks of astonishment infuriated me. Surely they didn't think I should excuse Mutti's violence because she'd suffered?

'I don't believe a word you've said!' I headed for the door.

'Look.'

I wheeled around as Mutti pulled up the sleeve of her cardigan. Near the inside crook of her left arm was a black tattoo I hadn't noticed before. Perhaps she'd always worn long sleeves. I peered. It read *B–32325*. 'What is it?'

'You had to show your number to get food. They made me believe I was a number.'

'Were you in Auschwitz?' I was awed.

Her eyebrows shot up. 'How do you know that name?'

'It's famous.'

'Infamous,' Mum said. Mutti looked like she didn't grasp the distinction.

My eyes were fixed on the floor. I was ashamed of how nasty I'd been. There wasn't very much worse that could happen to a person than what had happened to Mutti.

Chapter Eight

The essay question I chose for the history exam that came the next morning was about the Dissolution of the Monasteries in the 1530s and 1540s during the reign of Henry VIII. It was a turbulent time when the monks and nuns had to decide whether to give up like victims or fight back with zero chance of winning through. I thought of Mutti in Auschwitz and concluded that in the circumstances, to survive was to win.

After a break came the algebra I had tried to prepare for the previous night. It went rather well, I thought, considering I'd not done a whole lot of revision.

After lunch we could study in the library or go home a good two hours earlier than usual, which meant that things were relatively quiet in town. Only mums pushing prams and old ladies with shopping baskets were out and about.

I was thinking about the three further exams I needed to prepare for the next day – geography, English literature and Latin – when footsteps thudded on the pavement behind me. I turned to see Peter with his arms wrapped around his briefcase, grinning all over his face as he scooted towards me. The boy had no idea how to look hip. It was endearing.

'Where's the fire?' I asked, as he fell into step alongside of me.

What if he'd replied, 'In my heart'? What then?

'Ha, ha.' Not surprisingly, he was out of breath. 'How's life at the asylum?'

It was my turn to go, 'Ha, ha.' We girls were constantly getting teased about our school's temporary lodgings at the city's former mental hospital, where pupils had been receiving their education since getting bombed out in the 1942 air raids.

'And how was the algebra exam?'

'How do you know I just had algebra?' Did he have extrasensory perception?

'I saw Babs at the bus stop.'

My smile left me. 'Oh, well. It's a free country.'

'What do you mean?'

'Nothing. Algebra wasn't too bad.'

'That's not what she said.'

'I expect not.' Babs was in division three for maths. 'Did you have an exam?' I asked this because he was coming home early too.

'No, special science talk.'

'Yuck.' I wasn't sure why I said this. I didn't mind science.

'Yeah,' he agreed, though I suspected he was a whizz at it. 'So, how's your secret mother?'

'Shh!' Luckily, no one was within earshot.

'Oh, come on, Marlene.'

'You didn't tell Babs. Did you?'

'Course not.'

'Good.'

We sauntered through twisting streets close to the cathedral, past higgledy-piggledy old shops like Deakin's – with its window of gents' clothes and a second of school uniforms – Kennedy's shoes and Mears hardware, all long-established, though not as ancient as their buildings. This bit of town was mostly built around the time of the Dissolution of the Monasteries.

Peter wasn't going to let it go. 'Why don't you want Babs to know?'

What was this fixation with her?

'When I'm ready, *I'll* tell her.'

He nodded. 'Fair enough.'

That wouldn't be anytime soon. I didn't want it flying all around the school that I was an outsider, any more than I wanted his mother blabbing to the whole of Lanfranc Close about it. 'It's no one else's business.'

'Fair enough.'

'Shut up, Peter!'

He looked wounded. I didn't mean to hurt his feelings. I felt bad. 'Mutti's had a hard time of it, Peter. She was in a concentration camp, where she nearly died. Our whole family was wiped out. After the war, she went to Israel. But the *British* put her in a detention camp! Can you believe that?'

'Oh, yes,' he said, like he knew that had gone on.

I sent him a sideways look. The boy was encyclopaedic. 'She says even the kibbutz where she lives is a kind of camp.'

'I'm sure you'd love it, though.'

A lump came unexpectedly to my throat. Would I love it? 'I don't know. I don't know anything any more.' I felt lost.

'It'll be alright, Marlene.'

'Shut up, Peter. Even you don't know that!'

He looked hurt again. 'I was only trying to help.'

'I know.'

We were passing one of the postage-stamp-sized parks that were to be found all over Canterbury. This one was not much bigger than my front room at home.

'Come on.' Peter went in and sat on the bench.

'I've got revision,' I said, following him in.

We sat in silence in the little walled garden, listening to pigeons cooing in the magnolia tree beside us and breathing in the heady fragrance of its flowers. Fallen petals were spread around our feet like confetti.

I stretched my legs out straight in front of me. 'I don't think Mutti loves anyone but herself. It's not her fault. She just can't.'

I turned my ankles left and right, staring at my white socks and scuffed buckle shoes. 'I suppose the war was really hard on Mum too. She lost Dad and she lost the farm… But she's such a cold fish.' My sigh became a sob that turned into heaving sobs. The park misted like a rained-on watercolour.

Peter produced a folded hankie. 'Take it.' The letter 'P' was embroidered in blue in one corner. I was hesitant. 'It's clean.'

'Thanks.' I dabbed my eyes and blew my nose. I liked how it smelled of ironed linen. 'I'm sorry to be such a baby.'

'Look what you've been through, Marlene, and what you're still going through. From the start, your life was filled with uncertainty and fear. Next you were torn, without warning, from your mother and everything you knew. It's hardly surprising that you blocked out the memory of all that when you began to feel safe here. Now it's back to haunt you.'

'Don't,' I said. 'You'll set me bawling again... Did I tell you all this?'

'Some of it I pieced together.' His hazel eyes looked olive in the garden's green light. 'You tell me about Mutti and about your mum, but I think *you're* brave.'

'You do?' I winced under the intensity of his gaze.

The war hadn't been a bed of roses for anyone, including Peter, whose family's previous home had burned down during the bombardments of 1942.

'Yes. You're the one who's had it hardest of all.' He placed his hand on my shoulder and prayed that all would work out well for me.

Chapter Nine

I touched Peter's hankie in my pocket, as I stepped indoors feeling something approaching serene. That changed as soon as I saw Mum's face.

'What's up?' I dropped my satchel on the floor and hung my panama and blazer on the coat stand.

Mutti appeared from the back room. 'You still have Lottie, your big love doll?'

'Yes.'

Mum's voice was strained. 'Your mother as much as ordered me to bring her down.'

My eyes narrowed. She was a fine one to complain; she'd brought all this trouble on herself. And on me.

'She was so precious,' Mutti said, in a voice like she was stroking a kitten. 'But I couldn't find her. Where is she?'

She couldn't find her because I'd hidden her. I didn't know why. Something more that I didn't know I knew, perhaps? 'You went in my room?'

Mum said, 'I found her snooping around in there.'

Mutti pursed her lips, a petulant little girl. 'I want to see her.'

'I'll go and get her.' To show my displeasure, I stamped up the stairs. In the box room, where I'd been sleeping since Mutti came to stay, I gently released Lottie from her hiding place between the upright pillows and the quilted headboard at the top of the narrow bed. I came down with her tucked under my arm – like I used to when I was little. Mutti was looking perky. Mum, on the other hand, was pale.

'Ach!' Mutti smiled broadly. 'Everywhere you were, there too was *kleine Puppe Lottie.*'

It suddenly hit me that my doll was the *only* material link between Mutti and me. How sad to think that she was all that glued us together. Lottie was a poor old thing, but I loved her deeply; a lot more, if I was honest, than either mother right now.

My two mothers followed me into the back room. Sunlight was flooding in through the French windows, giving the specks of grey dust dancing in the air a ghostly look.

Mutti stretched eager arms. 'Give me.'

'Sit.' I indicated the armchairs either side of the fireplace. They sat. I sat on the couch between them and leaned forward. We looked like we were about to play pass the parcel.

'Did I name her after my cousin?'

'Of course.' Mutti sounded rattled.

For the first time since all this began, I experienced a pang of loss for the cousin I must have been close to. I leaned across and placed Lottie in Mutti's lap.

She fussed over her. 'She is so dirty. And she has only one eye.'

'She's One-Eyed Lottie.' I was already itching to take her back.

'She arrived with Marlene like that,' Mum said in a flat voice.

'Ach, *ja*! I remember. She lost her eye in Germany.' Laughing, Mutti ran her fingers over the stitches on Lottie's eye. 'That is my sewing. *Schrecklich. Nicht*?'

She was right, her stitches were awful. They looked like huge, haphazard eyelashes. Yet they were part of Lottie's charm.

Mutti continued chuckling to herself. 'The eye is lost with your memories, Lena.'

Mum and I exchanged glances. We didn't see what was funny.

To my horror, Mutti began to yank on the black thread around Lottie's eye patch. I couldn't believe what she was doing. I reached forward to try to stop her, but Mum got there first. She made a grab for Lottie and caught her leg.

'Stop it!' she ordered, all trace of apathy gone. 'Stop it, right now!' She tried to pull Lottie from Mutti's grasp, but Mutti held on, grim-faced.

My hands flew to my mouth in horror. Now Mum was pulling and Mutti was pulling back.

'*Lass mich,*' Mutti growled in her throaty voice. 'Let go!'

'Stop it!' Mum shouted. '*You* let go.'

I looked on helplessly as my doll stretched, thin and long, afraid to intervene and make matters worse than they already were. This tug-of-war could only end one way that I could see.

I was soon proved right. As the stitches attaching Lottie's leg to her body parted from the worn-out fabric of her belly, Mum was thrown backwards into the armchair, waving Lottie's leg. My doll's belly split open from end to end, releasing fluffy kapok stuffing that wafted into the room. At the same time, Mutti, who was also thrown backwards, lost her grip on what was left of Lottie, who flew through the air and landed on the carpet behind Mutti's chair with her body at right angles to her remaining leg.

I got to my feet to stand like a statue, with my hands clasped over my mouth, too shocked even to cry. Stuffing floated down like snow onto the carpet and the pale green lino that bordered it. Lottie was a broken corpse, with stuffing oozing out like intestines and her patched eye gaping.

Mum thrust down the limb in her hand as if it burned. She sent me a look of immense sorrow. I hated that look. 'Marlene, I'm so sorry.'

She was so smarmy, it made me sick. I mean really sick. My chest was heaving. I wanted to run to the bathroom, but I held it down and stayed.

'Perhaps I can put her back...' She got down on her hands and knees to gather Lottie up.

But Mutti lunged from her chair to grab Lottie. She peeled back my doll's eye patch to tug at something beneath and pulled out an object that flashed spangles of rainbow light onto the mirror above the mantelpiece. It was a bracelet that sparkled like diamonds.

'Are they real?' Mum asked, in a hushed voice.

They looked real to me, a chain of diamonds set in gold. But then I'd never seen real diamonds, except in the jeweller's window.

'Oh, yes,' Mutti replied, breathing hard.

Oh, golly gosh! Real diamonds.

'They belonged to my mother – to your Oma, Lena. She wanted you to have them.'

That was odd, I thought, seeing as she'd disowned me. I wondered if my Oma had wanted to make amends. Or maybe she had a better idea of what was coming than Mutti had implied. But then, why me and not my cousin Lottie, Rifka's daughter, who wasn't illegitimate?

I thought Mutti would hand the bracelet to me but, sitting up on her haunches, it was her own wrist she wound it around. She closed the clasp. Smiling to herself, she got to her feet and left the room.

Chapter Ten

An hour later, Mutti stood at the top of the stairs, wearing her tight black skirt and the cherry-red top that matched her lips and nails. Oma's bracelet was on her wrist. I had to wonder, as I looked up from the hallway below, whether she had come to England for me or for the diamonds. Me, I hoped. I only noticed the green canvas suitcase with the stickers of exotic-sounding names as she bent to pick it up. My heart started thudding.

'Are you going?'

She picked her way down the stairs in her high heels, placed the case by the door and took my hands in hers. 'Lena.' She pulled me to her and held me tight. 'I go back to Israel.'

'You can't leave me.'

'I cannot stay here with her.' She indicated Mum, who had come into the hallway from the back room. 'You could have told Lena you didn't know where her mother was. You could have said, "Perhaps she's dead," but you didn't. You pretended you were the mother.'

Mum shook her head. 'She never asked.'

Fire surged through me. Mum was forcing me to take sides. 'You kept me totally in the dark! You usurped my real mother and now she's leaving, and I'll never get to know her.'

Mutti stroked my hair. '*Wenn Du wohl weisst wer Du bist*... if you know who you really are, Lena, you'll come with me.'

'You only came for the bracelet.'

Mutti shook her head. 'No. I came to find you. And look who I found, a beautiful young woman.'

The intensity of her gaze made me squirm. I stared at the abstract brown wheels on the hallway carpet. 'You beat me.'

She shrugged 'That was the past. I too have grown up.'

At once, I knew that if I did not seize this opportunity – if I let Mutti go – I'd never know who I really was. And I would regret it forever. I smiled at Mutti. 'I'll come with you.'

They both seemed surprised. Mum had a sharp intake of breath.

'But you don't have a passport.' Mutti laughed.

'Yes, I do.' I had been on the school Outward Bound trip to Amiens in France the previous year. 'So, can I go, Mum?'

Mum looked dismayed.

'Isn't that for me to say?' Mutti said. 'I am your mother.'

Mum blinked. 'I wasn't expecting this right now. I think we should discuss it.'

She went back into the back room, but Mutti stood her ground. 'What's to discuss?' she called. 'She wants to come with me.'

Mum poked her head around the corner of the door. 'Can you pay her fare?' Silence. 'I thought not.'

We followed her in and sat in our usual places, my mothers on either side of the fireplace and me in between.

'So,' Mum said to me, 'the best thing would be to withdraw your savings from the Trustee Savings Bank.'

I'd put in a shilling a week, which they collected at my primary school every Monday. Since then, Mum had been making my weekly deposits when she did the shopping. I did a quick calculation in my head and turned to Mutti. 'Would about £17 be enough?'

'We must get the overnight train to Paris from Dover Marine, then a cab to the Gare de Lyon. We will take the new Mistral train to Marseille, and from there a ship for Haifa. We have to eat on the way.'

It sounded out of this world. 'What ports do we call at?'

Mutti didn't seem to find this very important. She waved away my question. 'Naples, I suppose.'

'Italy!' I told Mum.

'Or Piraeus, in Greece,' Mutti said. 'Maybe Nice first also... I think £17 would be too little.'

What an adventure! But I couldn't afford it. 'That won't cover it, Mum.'

Mum said, 'You have more than £17, Marlene.'

'I do? How come?'

She rummaged in her purse and brought out my tattered Trustee Savings Bank account book. She opened it and said, 'You have £61, ten shillings and eight pence.'

A small fortune! 'That's more than enough. Right?'

Mutti nodded.

'What's important,' Mum said, 'is that you have enough to get home again if you need to.'

Mutti looked like she'd sucked on a lemon. 'Why would she need to?'

'She might *want* to come home.'

'How did I get so much?'

'I've been adding to it when I could. I was thinking it would make a bit of a dowry for you when you got married.' Mum sighed. 'It's your money, Marlene, to do with as you like.'

'So, I can go to the South of France and sail to Israel and see some of those other places?'

'If that is your choice. Is that your choice?'

Of course it was my choice. I wasn't going to be answering questions about Shakespeare tomorrow or going to church next Sunday. I was going off to see the world!

The next few hours were a flurry of activity. We got to the Trustee Savings Bank branch in the centre of town just before it closed. After that, we went to the travel agency – where a lady with a pince-nez added my passage to Mutti's return ticket – then rushed back to pack and try to force some supper down.

Waiting for our train on the platform at Canterbury East station, it was hard to believe I wasn't just here to wave Mutti off; I was actually going somewhere. I was leaving all I could see in front of me: the city wall with the Dane John Gardens behind it, the Norman castle in ruins and the two great gasometer tanks, surrounded by metal cages, going up and down hypnotically on rollers as they filled and emptied gas from the gasworks. I knew almost nothing about my destination. Was I scared? Not so much of going as of having chosen wrongly.

The train pulled noisily into the station, brakes squealing and smoke billowing from the locomotive, making the platform look like a fog scene in a war movie. It brought with it a strong smell of sulphur and tar. I picked up my little suitcase, ready to get on, though it hadn't yet come to a halt. Mutti looked truly happy to see me so eager. Her eyes sparkled.

My suitcase was the same one I had arrived with in June 1939, eleven years earlier, almost to the day. Into it I had squeezed my non-school summer skirt, a couple of shirts, the new cream cardigan Mum had knitted me for summer, my shorts, regulation swimming costume and cap, and my plimsolls, socks, pyjamas and knickers. A hairbrush, toothbrush, toothpaste and bar of soap were in the green plastic toiletry bag. Oh, and I'd packed my Bible, which had made me think of Peter, just for a moment. So, I'd added his hankie.

In my white clutch purse were my tickets, passport and £1, ten shillings and eight pence. This would more than cover my food for the journey as far as Marseilles, Mum said. She gave into Mutti's safekeeping what she called the just-in-case money remaining after paying my fare – in case I wanted to come home. We had bought a one-way only ticket, since a return I might never use would have been very expensive, we discovered.

My little purse matched my Sunday pillbox hat. I also had on my ruby-red Sunday dress with the swirly skirt and a snake belt at the waist. On my feet were black patent pumps with kitten heels and draped over my arm was my navy school mac. With my hair loose about my shoulders, I felt quite the lady.

Doors to carriages opened and people got off the train. The sooty-faced driver leaned out of the engine, wiping his hands on a dirty rag. He grinned at everyone, seemingly happy in his work.

Mum took Mutti's hand and shook it. 'Take good care of Marlene.'

'I may not be the perfect mother,' Mutti replied with a nod, 'but I am the mother.'

The train was keeping up a slow pant. Mum turned to me. I put my suitcase down on the platform and stepped forward to hug her goodbye. At this point, there was an unexpected development. The excited anticipation of a moment before became porridge in my belly, stirred with a wooden spoon. Fear of the unknown could have been the cause, but since Mum seemed to be trembling too, it might have been something else entirely.

'Be a good girl.'

'I will.'

She smiled. 'Now, go on. Get on the train.'

I picked up my case and watched myself step on after Mutti. I tugged the door behind me so it slammed shut. Mum waved as I pulled down the window.

Though my legs were shaking, everything else was curiously still and lost in time. Mutti settled herself in; I remained standing. Every sound but my breath, keeping time with that of the engine, was muffled. In slow motion, I put my hand through the window to grasp Mum's, but the guard's whistle speeded everything up. Her head turned in his direction, she stepped back, he waved his flag, and with a long 'shoo' of steam pressure and a grinding of the wheels, the carriage lurched forward and the train gave a piercing whistle. We were off.

My teeth felt cold and cluttered in my mouth. My lips quivered. I wanted to cry, 'I love you!' But I didn't. I didn't say anything. I watched as Mum stood with one hand raised, until she looked no bigger than a doll's house person, until we rounded a bend and lost sight of the platform.

Chapter Eleven

'It's something special. Isn't it?'

I turned from leaning on the ship's railing to acknowledge the elderly man who had spoken to me. He wore pebble glasses like they used to during the war. He was plump and hairy, with a long beard, and thick tufts of grey and reddish hair trying to escape from under his black homburg hat. He was referring to the view.

This was my first glimpse of Israel and I was awed. 'Yes. Breathtaking.'

The blue waters of the broad bay our ship was entering were rimmed by an arc of golden sands. Clusters of white houses climbed the steep slopes that rose behind the shore, backed by mountains of ginger and sage that seemed to go on forever. I could do anything I set my mind to in such an inspiring place, I felt, and be whoever I might turn out to be.

The old man leaned against the railing beside me and smiled. There was something gentle and cheery about his manner. 'Is this the first time you are in Israel?'

'Yes. Do you live here?'

He nodded. 'Since 1946.'

'What's it like?'

'Hot.'

We both laughed.

It was warm enough here on deck. The heat that seemed to be rising from the deck's planks was augmented by the crowd of people. All around us was an expectant buzz. Many of the passengers were about to make a new beginning, like me.

At the dock, little dots of people waiting to meet them seemed to be waving and shouting, though they were too far away to be heard. I probably wouldn't understand them anyway. On board, I'd heard any number of languages. Doubtless, it would be the same story on dry land.

There were men and women of all ages, from babies to pensioners. Some had long beards and dusty black suits. Mutti called all of them 'rabbis'. Most looked like people everywhere. Only chiselled cheekbones and jawlines and an unfamiliar cut to their clothing set them apart from anyone you might come across in England.

'The best thing about Israel,' my new friend said, 'is that everyone else is Jew also. You are not going to receive any bad looks from your neighbours as you go to buy food or to the post office.'

'Are you German?' I asked, picking up on his accent.

'Oh no!' He pulled a wry face. 'I am from another land the Nazis took over, Hungary. But in my heart, I am a *Sabra,* a born Israeli.'

'You sound like Mutti when you speak.'

'The lady I have seen you with on the ship,' he replied, 'she speaks German like the Germans. I speak Yiddish.'

I shook my head. I had never heard of Yiddish.

'It is the Jewish language.'

'I thought that was Hebrew.'

'Also,' he conceded with a grin.

As the ship slowed and the shoreline grew bigger, the wind that had been strong on my face throughout the voyage slackened off, allowing me to smell the briny sea. The activity of passengers and crew, as well as those on shore, grew more frenzied.

I was obliged to shout above the noise. 'I only just found out I'm Jewish.'

'It happens – the war. And the *Shoah*.'

'What's that?'

'The Holocaust.'

'What does it mean to be Jewish?'

He shrugged. 'Trouble. Always trouble.'

I wasn't sure what to make of that.

Some people behind us began singing a rousing Jewish song called *Hava Nagila* and dancing in a circle while onlookers clapped their hands and joined in. The old man's eyes twinkled as he tapped his foot in time to the music. His words gave the lie to his demeanour, however. 'Most of these happy immigrants are about to spend six months or more living in tents in holding camps. It will not be easy. Israel has not enough houses for all the Jews pouring in. You too?'

'No. I am going to a kibbutz with Mutti.'

'*Mazal tov.*' In answer to my puzzled frown, he added, 'It means "congratulations".'

'Thank you.'

We were about to dock. I looked up at the hills and wondered if Jesus ever walked where my eyes were falling.

This country was, after all, where He had lived. I thought of Peter, who would love this, and wondered what he might be doing right now: sleeping, no doubt, for it was still early and English time was even earlier.

I turned to the old man. 'Could I ask you something?'

'Of course.'

I led him by the sleeve a little astern, away from the hubbub. 'Can I be a Jew and believe in Jesus?'

He looked a little surprised. 'Not if you want other Jews to like you.'

'Why don't Jews believe in Jesus?'

'He was an imposter.'

'How do you know?'

'How do *you* know he was the Messiah?'

'Because he rose from the dead.'

The old man looked like he didn't think that was very likely.

'More than 500 people saw him,' I said.

'Let us agree to disagree. For now.'

He produced a business card from his inside jacket pocket and handed it to me. 'If you ever want to talk about these things – or anything else – you can come and find me.'

I looked at it. It was written in Hebrew. Suddenly, I realised I was going to be illiterate.

Noticing my look of despair, he said, 'It says Rav Shlomo Liebermann.'

'Rav?'

'Rabbi.'

'You're a rabbi?'

The other rabbis on board had seemed unapproachable, looking the other way and freezing us out whenever we were around them.

'Rabbi Shlomo Liebermann.'

'Pleased to meet you. I'm Lena Levi.' There! I'd owned my name.

'Pleased to meet you, Miss Lena Levi.'

I extended my hand to shake his, but his didn't move from his side. So, I sent mine on up and scratched my nose instead, hoping he hadn't noticed.

Below us, the crew lowered the gangplank to cheers all around. The first passenger to disembark went down on his face and kissed the quay. This was soon followed by emotional reunions, tears, laughter, hugs like people would never let go, greetings in assorted languages and more ground-kissers.

It all seemed at once over the top and moving. I told myself I should tear myself away and go to find Mutti. At that very moment, she appeared on deck and came over to us. With a nod to the rabbi, she casually put her arm around my waist, like we belonged to one another. This still seemed strange, but I was growing used to it.

'Are you ready, *schatzi*?'

'Yes, let's go,' I said.

PART TWO

Chapter Twelve

ISRAEL, JULY 1950

I had worked in the nursery almost every day since my arrival at Kibbutz Eshkadosh a month before. Right then, I was helping little Uri, who was having a fine old time with his painting, making the paper colourful, along with his arms, legs and face. I wasn't very strict with the tinies, but that didn't seem to matter here. The children were cuddled and indulged. They could do exactly as they pleased, including running off in all directions.

'Lena!'

The voice calling me was that of the kibbutz director, Dov. The two other nursery assistants in the room smiled at him. He was a handsome man in his mid-twenties, with black curls, dark skin and startling green eyes. He was also mysterious, with a recent past in the Israeli Army he refused to talk about.

'Can you come and make your *aliyah* application now?' he asked me.

Aliyah, which means 'going up', was the lovely expression they used for immigration, evoking pilgrims of old who would sing psalms as they made their way up the steep mountainside to Jerusalem to worship at the temple on Jewish festivals.

'Ooh, yes!' I couldn't wait to become a bona fide Israeli.

'Come, then.'

Dov was the only one here apart from Mutti who spoke to me in English and, therefore, the only one I understood. Everyone else spoke to me in Hebrew. I was just starting to pick up a few phrases, especially from the children.

I told my young artist how well he'd done: '*Tov*, Uri. *Tov meod*.'

I went through to the next room to tell Sara, who was in charge of the nursery, 'Dov wants me.'

'*Yesh luckh mazal*,' she drawled, as if talking were too much trouble. Sara always behaved like she couldn't be bothered with anything. She got a surprising amount done, considering.

I had no idea what her words meant.

Her '*L'hitraot*' – see you later – I got, though it was followed with further unfamiliar gibberish.

I thought she meant I shouldn't be too long as I was needed to help with the children's supper. All the children here lived with us leaders. Parents had only a short time with them in the evenings, before they returned to sleep in dormitories, under our supervision. Every day after supper was my time off too. I spent it with Mutti – although now she wanted me to call her Imma.

As I returned to Dov in the other room, I thought that Sara might have said something else entirely. I could end up the laughing stock as I often had been already, when I took guesses at what people here were telling me.

'What does *yesh luckh mazal* mean?' I asked him, as I opened and shut the children's safety gate and he led the way down the stairs. No 'ladies first' here.

'Lucky you.'

Like everyone else, Sara must have a bit of a crush on Dov. I know I did.

The tiny hint of a breeze coming in through the upstairs windows was absent in the red dirt compound outside. Before we reached the office-cum-café 100 yards away, my shirt was sticking to my back and underarms.

Inside, the wooden hut was sweltering. Perspiration beaded on my face and ran down as Dov brought iced water from the refrigerator. Back in England, we didn't have a refrigerator, let alone iced water. I gulped it down.

He sat opposite me. There were dark rings of sweat around the armpits of his shirt. He slid a form across the table. The table was covered with yellow Formica, just like Mum's kitchen table at home.

At first, the form looked impossible. It was written in Hebrew. But with a month of working my way through the *Kadimah Introduction to Hebrew* under my belt, I found I could make out where they wanted me to put my name, address, date and place of birth. Writing answers to these questions, however, would be another matter entirely.

He picked up on my helpless expression. 'I'll help you fill it out. Did you know they just passed the Law of Return?'

'No. What is it?'

'It confirms your right to be a citizen of Israel, the home of your ancestors, since you are Jewish.'

It struck me now that I was family to every Jewish character in the Bible, which was almost all of them. Gosh, I could be a direct descendent of Mary, the mother of Jesus, who was Jewish too.

But this connection seemed surreal, like I was only pretending to be a Jew.

'Now, what about your name?' Dov was saying.

'My legal name? It's Marlene Roberts.'

'Levi.'

'My passport says Roberts.'

'Your mother's name is Levi.' He wrote it down. And just like that, he made me Lena Levi in real life.

'You might want to change your first name,' he said.

'Why?'

'To sound more Israeli. I was not Dov in Iran. I was Farhad. Dov is my Hebrew name, like King David, you know? You could use yours.'

This was a novel idea. 'Do I have one?'

'Don't you know it?'

'No.'

'Didn't Rochel give you a Hebrew name at birth?'

He called Mutti by her first name. Here, everyone seemed to be on a first-name basis. It was a lot less formal than England.

He waved his pen, determined to write something, it seemed. 'Would you like to use a different name as an Israeli citizen?'

I was feeling pressured. 'I'd like to ask Imma.'

I could see he found me tiresome.

'Is that alright?'

'How old are you?'

He knew how old I was. He'd just written down my date of birth and hadn't even noticed that my birthday was Christmas Day. Everyone always noticed that.

'In a year and a half, you'll be in the army,' he said. 'Then you will be facing situations you cannot go ask your imma about.'

He was so unfair. I was in a strange country with strange ways. I thought I was doing well. I didn't want him to see my hurt, so I scraped back my chair. 'I'll go and ask her now.' I was already on my way. 'Thanks for your help.'

'We'll continue Sunday.' In Israel, Sunday was like Monday, a workday. '*Shabbat shalom.*' This meant, 'Have a peaceful Sabbath.' It was Friday evening and the Sabbath would come in at dusk and last until sunset on Saturday.

'Shabbat shalom,' I echoed as I went out of the door, feeling anything but peaceful.

Grumbling to myself about Dov, I headed for the covered cattle pens. I had been shocked to learn when I first came here that I would have to serve in the army. In England, only boys did that. But I had got used to the idea. I was even looking forward to wearing beige fatigues and carrying a rifle or machine gun, like all the kids here. No doubt I would know the Hebrew for 'run' and 'duck' by the time I was drafted.

There was no sign of Mutti among the stalls of cute calves that smelled of pee-sodden straw. Fending off flies, I went into the gloom of the milking shed behind. I made out three milkmaids in headscarves, none of them her. One asked me if I was looking for Rochel.

'*Ken,*' I affirmed.

I wasn't expecting to understand her response, but it was so simple, even I got it.

'Hee b'har.' She was on the mountain. She would be watching the cows and bulls turned out to graze up there.

I started back in the direction of the tinies' building and my duties there, but the mountain beckoned. Dov thought I couldn't do things by myself. But I could. I was the intrepid traveller who'd taken herself off, alone, to explore Naples when Mutti hadn't felt like it. I'd learned that Roman history was wonderful, but that Italian men were stalkers. I'd survived that. Now I would show Dov. I would go and keep Mutti company while she watched the livestock, and find out what my Hebrew name was. I hadn't once been for a walk since I got here. It was something I missed. Back in Canterbury I walked everywhere.

So, plan made, I veered off towards the rows of terraced bungalows where most kibbutzniks lived. These were very plain but arranged around a lovely grassed quadrangle, lined with eucalyptus, flame trees and purple-flowered bougainvillea. I passed the back of the canteen with the nursery upstairs and the children's playground below, with its swings and slide. I passed the turquoise swimming pool that was walled on three sides. It was deserted. Everyone was still at work. Everything was still but for the fluttering of birds' wings and the lazy buzzing of bees.

Originally a religious kibbutz, it was now predominantly secular. There would be worship this evening in the canteen, ahead of the special meal we always ate on the Sabbath, but hardly anyone attended. I did once and was the only girl. It hadn't felt like God was there, not for me at least. It didn't help that I couldn't understand a word, but I didn't see how the others could either, the way they were tearing through the pages in a hurry to be done.

I reached the high, wire-meshed perimeter fence. The barrier at the rear gate was raised to allow the kibbutz farm traffic to come and go. I waved to Dov's father, Yaacov, up in the watchtower, but he was chuckling to himself as he read a comic and didn't see me. It felt liberating to step across the threshold into the pomegranate groves, with the open countryside beyond. The trees here offered some shade from the dazzling sun and seemed to give off a little cool air of their own.

Peter, who'd replied to my letter explaining where I was, assumed I'd be learning to prune vines and shear sheep. His biblical bias to everything was funny, as if this country was locked in time and still as it was 2,000 years before.

Our farming methods here were right up-to-date. Our orchards were turned over to oranges and lemons, as well as pomegranates, and our banana plantation stretched to the rim of the high plateau on which the kibbutz stood. A forest of saplings – acacia, cedar, pine and others – grew on the steep slopes that surrounded us. We were growing trees, lots of them. And we had beef cattle up on the mountain, with dairy below in the compound.

Peter's letter wasn't romantic or anything, but he'd signed it, 'Chin up! Peter', like he knew it was a bit tough for me here. And he'd added an 'x'. So, I kept it under my pillow when I slept.

A ditch marked the boundary of the pomegranate orchard. It was overgrown with tall cacti, to help keep the wild animals out. There were hyena and jackal and wild boar in this country.

There were also vipers. So, I kept my eyes peeled as the track zig-zagged steeply upwards. I was feeling a strong pull on my behind and a drag on my knees with every step. And boy, was I sweating! There was little shade here among the scrub and carob trees hung with their long black pods. A rhythmic pounding in my head soon began to mark time with the throbbing harmonies of all kinds of bugs. I thought about turning back. But I had a point to make.

A Jewish settlement came into view below the juvenile forest at my feet. The blue-and-white Israeli flag was flying on a pole at its centre. As I climbed further, flat-roofed houses of Arab villages on the mountainside opposite came into view, divided from us by the main road that ran like a ribbon through the valley below.

I was now high enough to see the Technion behind me. This was the elite university where Dov hoped one day to study engineering. Beyond that lay Haifa, its buildings white in the sunlight and spilling down to the Mediterranean.

I had been to Haifa only once since our ship docked there, and was surprised to find its shops ramshackle and its colonial houses crumbling, while cranes threw up boxy apartment buildings. What a let-down after the city had appeared so alluring from the water.

One thing I had noticed about Israel: the close-up details of daily life might be ordinary in their way, even if they were different from England. Yet, from time to time, something in the atmosphere would grab me and I would look around at the landscape and be filled with a sense of wonder to be here, in the Holy Land, where God seemed especially present. At that moment, it was quite possible to believe I might run into Jesus Himself, coming down the stony track to meet me.

As I stood, getting my breath back, I became aware of the whining of a vehicle on the track below me. It was raising a trail of dust. The sound became louder until a military-looking jeep loomed at my back. It was khaki, with a canvas canopy, one of those Second World War models with an engine louder than a flight of bomber planes. As it screeched to a halt alongside me, I was enveloped in a cloud of ginger dust that clogged my nostrils and prickled in my eyes. Dov was at the wheel.

'Get in, now!'

His tone didn't allow for questions. I got straight in. I sat in the solitary back seat. Little Uri's dad, I didn't know his name, was sitting beside Dov in front with a rifle stood between his legs. Dov threw the jeep into gear. The tyres spun and we shot forward.

'What the hell do you think you're doing?'

He was being very rude, I thought. 'Going to see my mother.'

He glared at me in the mirror. '*Meshugenah* – are you crazy?'

I didn't know what to say. I sat up very straight and stared pointedly out at the mountains. I was half expecting a tirade from Dov, but he didn't say another word as he turned the steering wheel this way and that and tugged at the gearstick. As for Uri's father, he didn't so much as glance in my direction.

It was a bumpy ride to the top of the mountain, to say the least. With every stone, I bounced. With every bend rounded at top speed, I was thrown sideways. I kept blinking to try to clear the dust from my eyes.

Just shy of the very top, I was thrown forward as we stopped – dead – beside a shelter. It was more like a birdwatchers' hide or a bunker, really: breeze blocks piled up and cemented together in the shape of a flat-roofed, biblical-style house, with a wide slit for a window. All around it on the scrubby slopes were cowpats and grazing cattle. Uri's father got out, taking the rifle with him.

'Stay in the vehicle!' Dov ordered as I went to get out too.

I stayed in the vehicle. So did Dov. He grabbed a revolver from the door pocket and looked around him, scanning the slopes, with the engine idling.

Mutti came out of the shelter and scrunched a cigarette under her boot. Her everyday look here in Israel was nothing like she'd had in England. She was wearing khaki shorts, a man's military-style shirt, and a floppy hat. She too was carrying a rifle. She spoke to Uri's father for a moment, handed him a walkie-talkie and the binoculars hanging around her neck, and came to join us in the jeep. She didn't look at me either. The anger was rising inside me. This treatment wasn't fair.

Dov revved up the vehicle. I gritted my teeth in anticipation of our descent. This turned out to be even more hair-raising than I had feared. At one point, I shut my eyes and prayed. Silently.

Dov ranted at Mutti in Hebrew, all the way down. She responded curtly. Maybe three times, she affirmed, '*Ken.*'

I glimpsed the prickly pear cacti, the pomegranate orchard, and the barrier beneath Yaacov, still in the watchtower, as we sped past. We jolted to a halt by the lush grass of the quadrangle.

Mutti turned around to me. 'Come.'

She strode away in the direction of her bungalow, leaving me to clamber out, jelly-legged, avoiding eye contact with Dov. Clearly, I'd done something I should be ashamed of, though I failed to see what. Abruptly, he engaged the jeep's gears and drove off.

I wobbled along like a drunkard, fizzing inside after my ride. Mutti opened the door to her bungalow and went in. Nobody locked their doors here. No one had much to take, although we had her mother's bracelet, of course, which I supposed she had kept well hidden.

She held the door. I went in hesitantly, wondering what might be coming next. Inside, the bungalow was shadowy and close. It smelled of Mutti's perfume and stale cigarettes. The only light came from the half-open metal slats across the high window. There were twin beds, a wardrobe with drawers, a bedside table and lamp, a small desk and a chair. Everyone's furniture was the same. You went to the big hangar, picked out what you wanted, and carted it back to your bungalow.

Mutti shut the door behind me. 'Sit.'

I sat on the bed I seldom used because mostly I slept with the children.

She stood over me. 'So, it seems you've been bad.'

'But I don't know what I...' I broke off mid-sentence because, to my surprise, she was smiling.

'You should not go out alone.'

'Because of the wild animals?'

'You could call them that. Because of the snipers.'

'Snipers?' What was she talking about?

'In the Arab villages.' She demonstrated by taking aim and picking me off, though with her fingers rather than with her rifle, which she'd laid on her bed.

Relief washed over me. I had survived the danger I'd put myself in. Better still, Mutti wasn't being as vile to me as it had been plain Dov wanted her to be. I sent up another prayer, this one of thanks.

'You must not go off on your own. Sara was worried about you. No one could find you.'

'But how was I to know?'

She shrugged. 'This is Israel. Just last year we were at war.'

I hung my head, aware of how naïve and foolish I had been. And I'd put others at risk as they tried to protect me from my own recklessness. Even so, I was full of resentment because it clicked with me, at last, that I was a prisoner here, living surrounded by a high fence topped with barbed wire, banned from going out alone, even in broad daylight.

'Look, *schatzi...*'

A tingle of delight went through me every time she said that.

'... it is not an easy life here. And now you must pretend to Dov that I was very strict with you. And you must look after the babies tonight instead of coming to Shabbat supper.'

I would miss the best meal of the week. And I would miss *kiddush*, when wine and sweet *challah* bread were blessed and shared in a little ritual so similar to Christian Holy Communion that Jesus must surely have been inspired by it at the Last Supper.

I snorted, as if I didn't care about their punishment.

'As you must be on duty, you will miss the show.'

Friday evening Sabbath was an occasion for celebration, with singing and dancing after the meal, but a show was not the norm. I was crestfallen.

'I will perform. You won't see me.' She looked so disappointed that it seemed the punishment was even more on her than on me. 'I will sing *Bab el Wad*.'

'What's that?'

'You don't know *Bab el Wad*?' She looked as if the whole world should know it. 'Everyone cries when I sing it.'

'That bad, eh?'

We both laughed. It snapped the tension between us and things seemed alright again. She gave me an affectionate shove as she sat on the bed beside me.

'You know, I was very worried about you,' she said. 'We could see you coming up on foot and alone. It was madness.'

'I didn't know.' I steered the conversation back to her song. 'Aren't you going to tell me about... What is it, *Babby*?'

'Bab el Wad is a valley on the road up to Jerusalem.'

She got to her feet and began to sing the song to me, her audience of one. She marched up and down in the tiny room, giving the stirring song her all. They had excluded me from the Shabbat show. Yet here she was performing it, and here I was watching it anyway.

My applause as she finished was enthusiastic. 'Mutti, that was wonderful.'

Tears were in her eyes as she got her breath back.

'Imma,' she corrected.

I had wondered about her request for this change to Hebrew and come to the conclusion that it transformed us, in her estimation, from Holocaust survivors to Israeli pioneers and therefore from immigrant victims to go-getters who belonged. I liked the sound of that.

'The song is about the valley where the Arabs lay in wait for our convoys during the War of Independence,' she said. 'Many Jews died trying to deliver food and water and medicine to our people under siege in the Jewish Quarter of Jerusalem.'

'Oh.'

'Oh?' She gestured with her hands like she wanted me to react more strongly to her words, but I had no markers in my own history to connect them to. Leastways, none that I could remember.

'About today,' I said. 'I was coming up to ask you my Hebrew name.'

Her eyes widened in surprise. 'Your Hebrew name?'

'Yes, what is it?'

Clearly, it wasn't on the tip of her tongue. 'I suppose your Hebrew name could be your Oma's name, now that she is gone. It's Sara.'

'Like Sara, the children's leader?'

'Yes.'

I tried the name on for size. It didn't fit. I had thought a Hebrew name would give me a new, exciting persona. Instead, it felt like I was trying to muscle in on someone else's, whether Sara here or the grandmother I didn't remember, the one who'd thought Israel would be too hot to live in. She had a point, though. It was baking.

I was who I was, Marlene, after Marlene Dietrich, whose full name, I'd found out, was Marie Magdalene, or Marlene for short. I had to laugh because Mutti would never intentionally have named me after Mary Magdalene, one of the most famous Christians of all. I was also Lena. It was what everyone called me here. Two names were plenty. And two surnames were more than enough. There was no need to complicate things any further than they already were.

Chapter Thirteen

I was very excited to be outside the kibbutz, especially excited to be here in Nazareth, where Jesus grew up. The streets were full of all kinds of people wearing all kinds of clothes. Everyone was shouting, it seemed, even if they were just having a conversation, and car horns were joining in. My head was on a constant swivel.

I was here because I overheard Sara telling Dov she needed a see-saw for the tinies' playground. And he replied, 'I know a carpenter in Nazareth.' Well, of course I wanted to go too.

It had been a couple of weeks since Dov 'rescued' me from the mountain. We'd made a kind of peace, sufficient for him to complete my citizenship application and for me to beg him to bring me with him.

We had bundled into the kibbutz truck and in twenty minutes or so were parking outside the workshop of a Christian Arab named Youssef. His workshop was a cave-like room littered with tools, trestles and offcuts of wood and shavings that smelled deliciously nutty. It opened directly on to the street with fold-back wooden doors. I wondered if Jesus' own workshop looked similar to this one.

Dov discussed with Youssef what we needed and the two of us went for lunch at a roadside café. Dov ordered a revolting dish of beans called *ful* that all the way here he'd built up to me as something out of this world. He ate most of my portion, along with his own.

It still wasn't time to go back to Youssef's, even after sipping sweet mint tea out of little glasses that were too hot to hold. We got to our feet and started walking. Lining the busy street were makeshift cafés where men played cards or smoked water pipes. The passing handcarts and donkeys, bicycles and cars were throwing up the dust.

'This is the way to the souk.' Dov was trailing behind me with his hands in his pockets. 'It's worth a look.' The souk was the Arab market.

We climbed a hill and came alongside a large square church with a frontage of columns that put me in mind of a Greek temple. I stopped for a look.

'What are you doing?' Dov was clearly impatient.

'What is this place?'

'Some church.'

I was sure he knew full well that it was the world-famous Church of the Annunciation.

'Can we go in?'

His laughter was mocking. 'It's not for Jews.'

'I'm sure it's for everybody. I want to go in.'

'Come on. The souk is this way.' He carried on up the hill. But I approached the entrance and Dov turned back. He wasn't about to leave me on my own. A few days before, Arab guerrillas had shot an Israeli woman dead and wounded her boyfriend in an orange grove just south of Haifa.

A priest in a long white robe stepped out from the shadows, barring my way. 'You must cover your head and shoulders.' His English was strongly accented. He was Italian, perhaps, and pretty officious for someone I judged to be a young man.

'Oh, please, please let me in.' I tried to see past him.

He sniffed. 'And your legs.'

They were bare: I was wearing my blue shorts. He tucked himself back inside the porch. Dov was laughing. He thought he'd won. But I spotted a stall in the street, selling scarves. 'Buy me some of those.'

'I have no money.'

'Not true!' I said. 'You had money for lunch, a whole roll of notes. I've worked all summer and not received a bean. You can buy me some cheap scarves.' I went up to the stall and pulled out three plain cotton ones at random. They smelled musty. 'These won't break the bank.'

'Stop this.' His face was serious.

'Or else?'

'Why is this so important to you?' His eyes narrowed. 'Do you believe in Yeshu or something?'

'Yes, I do.' He stepped away from me like I had a disease.

'And it's not Yeshu but Yeshua.' That much I did know. The first was a curse, the second the Hebrew name for Jesus.

He lifted his hands to heaven. 'How can this be?' This was odd. To the best of my knowledge, he was as much an atheist as the rest of them at the kibbutz. He looked at me. 'Why?'

'Why what?'

'Why do you believe in him?'

This floored me momentarily, but I managed to find words I thought might be meaningful to him. 'Because he was the promised Messiah.'

The scarf vendor – a short woman in a shapeless black shift so long it draped on the ground – was growing impatient, shuffling her feet, speaking to me loudly in guttural Arabic and gesturing to give the scarves back.

'Are you going to buy these, or what?' I pushed them into Dov's hand.

He started haggling over the price with her in Arabic. She waved pudgy fingers at him. He waved back and pointed at a fourth scarf. He was trying he get four scarves for the price of three.

'What do you want an extra one for?' I asked.

'It's for my girlfriend.'

'You don't have a girlfriend.'

'I'll find one.'

I wanted to fire back, 'Who'd want *you*?' But I didn't. For he might just think *I* did and, handsome or not, he was way too grown-up for me. Eventually, he paid her and threw the scarves in my face.

'Go visit your Yeshu. I'll wait by the door.'

I wasn't about to thank him. He watched sulkily as I tied the black scarf around my hips. It hung to below my knees. I draped the green one over my shoulders. The maroon one I folded into a triangle and wore over my head.

'*Yaffa*,' he said.

'Thanks.' I was being sarcastic. The last thing I felt was pretty.

This time, the priest stood aside to let me in. I thought I heard him titter as I passed. And no wonder. I looked like a tramp about to do the Dance of the Seven Veils.

The lights inside the Church of the Annunciation were dim and the air was thick with the smell of candles and incense. The nave was filled with rows of benches that faced the grotto where the angel told Mary that she would have baby Jesus. This was flanked by stairs that led up to an altar on the top of the grotto. It was decked with all kinds of regalia – candelabra, silver ornaments, and statues of the Virgin Mary.

Groups of tourists were circulating. There was a line of people waiting to approach the grotto. I was disappointed. This was just another tourist place. Hardly anyone was sitting. Hardly anyone was praying.

I didn't know what I had been expecting, but it wasn't this. I sat on a bench and shut my eyes, wondering uneasily if I only believed in Jesus because Mum had always taken me to church, because we sang about Him at school assembly every morning. What if none of it was real? I had come here hoping to feel something special, like I had with Peter back in England when he prayed for me. But I was being assailed by doubts.

I still hoped, in spite of all. 'Please help me find You myself.' That was my prayer. I had nothing more to say. I remained seated with my head bowed.

Quiet stole over the church. The silence carried on it a kind of static. It made me open my eyes. To my amazement, I found I was quite alone. The tourists were gone. The priests too. I looked behind me. There was no one else in this massive space, where the angel Gabriel had once visited Mary. I smiled and closed my eyes again.

'You took your time.' Dov was leaning against a wall. 'We must get back to Youssef.'

I nodded. We set off down the hill.

He looked at me intently. 'You look different.'

'Different?'

'Your face is shiny.'

I grinned. 'I'm a new creation.' I was only half joking.

'You met your Yeshu?'

'Yeshua.'

'I don't believe in any of that.'

'Not even in the God of Israel?'

He looked edgy. 'I don't believe in anything.'

I was thinking about dropping this subject when he blurted, 'How can you call yourself a Jew when you worship Yeshu?'

And I retorted, 'How can you call yourself a Jew if you don't even believe in God?'

I realised from his expression that I'd gone too far. Nevertheless, the force of his reaction shocked me. He shoved me into the narrow alleyway alongside us and pinned me against the wall. His face, in mine, was nasty. 'You want to call yourself an Israeli. You're not fit to be an Israeli!'

I struggled to push him away, but it was getting me nowhere.

'Rivers of Jewish blood have been spilled so ungrateful traitors like you can come into this land and act like it's not good enough for them.'

My arms were hurting. 'Let me go!'

'Your so-called God just looks on as we fight and die!'

This didn't seem the best time to point out that it was illogical to complain about a God who didn't exist.

Instead, I stopped struggling and forced myself to go limp. Then I spoke in my most reasonable voice, hoping he wouldn't notice the tremor in it. 'Dov, let me go.' He released me then and backed away, covering his eyes with one hand.

I tugged at his arm. 'Youssef. We need to get back to Youssef.' He blinked at me, his face filled with pain.

What had happened? I wondered as we wended our way through cars and charabancs, braying donkeys and ever-milling crowds. What had I said or done to provoke such a violent reaction?

Chapter Fourteen

That evening I lay, hot and sweaty, in my bed in Mutti's bungalow, upset and confused by the way Dov had been with me. I was now also cross with Mutti, who wasn't here and had said she would be. I'd been here since just after supper, waiting.

After what seemed like hours of tossing and turning, the light clicked on and she breezed in. My eyes battled the blaze of light although, in truth, the bulb in the centre of the ceiling was feeble.

'A day such as this takes me back to how days used to be.' She was wearing her high heels, tight skirt, and cherry-red lipstick like she had in England.

I groaned. 'What time is it?'

Between the metal window slats, the night outside was black.

'Were you sleeping? Wake up.'

I sat up in the bed, still blinking. My skin was clammy. It was as hot as an oven in the bungalow. 'Where were you?'

'Look!' Mutti swung carrier bags of assorted sizes and colours onto my bed. Some bore bold designs, some had Hebrew store names on them, others were in English. It was like Christmas morning. 'I've been to Tel Aviv! They have real shops there.'

'So I see.' She might have taken me with her.

I'd told her I would be sleeping over tonight. I had been looking forward to it, despite how hard it was to find sleep in her stuffy bungalow in the late July heat, and despite her nightmares that always ended with screams that yanked me back to wakefulness.

I'd get up to comfort her. She'd twitch and murmur the names of the dead. Sometimes, these were nothing more explicit than 'the old man' or 'the woman with the baby', spoken in German. Her nights were an endless procession of these ghosts. It was like I was the mummy, then.

'There are lots of lovely things for you.' She rifled through the bags. 'What about this?' She tugged white tissue paper from a pink-striped bag. Peeling it back, she held up a dress. It was black and figure hugging with a wide belt of patent leather.

I frowned. 'It looks very grown-up.'

She laughed and draped it in front of her. 'Ach! This is not for you. This one is for me.' She laid it lovingly on her bed and began to undress. 'I'll show you.'

'Aren't you hot, Mutti?' It was close enough to suffocate.

'Imma,' she corrected. 'You'll get used to the climate, in time. I did.'

She put on the dress. 'Zip me up.' I got up and did as she asked.

The dress was low cut at the bodice and tight on the hips. I couldn't imagine any occasion at the kibbutz when she might wear it. She did a twirl before me, seemingly unaware of the numbers on her arm. Here in Israel she never tried to cover them up.

'You look so glamorous.'

She laughed, pleased. 'Let's have a fashion show.'

'But I'm all sweaty.'

'Go take a shower.'

'Now?'

'Yes, look.' She bent to pull out shorts and shirts, frilly undies and a white taffeta petticoat. 'These are for you.'

There was French perfume with matching soap and body lotion. There was costume jewellery and lingerie for her. Finally came the dress, the one that really got my attention. It was everything any girl my age would ever dream of wearing.

It was of blue sateen, the colour of the Mediterranean, with a flared skirt and cinched waist. The shoulders were cut away to a sailor collar in white that met in a 'V' at the front, where a single stone, sewn on to the fabric, glinted like a diamond.

'It looks expensive,' I said.

Anything looking that much like a Vogue design had to be.

'Nothing's too special for my little girl.' She rummaged through the bags again. 'There are some shoes to go with it somewhere.'

My eyes were still on the dress. 'I'll go and take a shower.'

This would involve scattering all the lizards along the shadowy path to the bathroom block that lay beside the main buildings. I reached for my towel on the towel rail.

'See the shoes.' She held them up. They were white heeled sandals. Really pretty.

I paused and looked back at her from the door. 'Mu–Imma, why didn't you tell me you were going?'

'Yaacov was going in the truck.' She ran her hands down her hips, admiring her own reflection in the narrow mirror on the wardrobe door. 'He asked me if I wanted to come. Who would say no to that?'

'Exactly. Who would?' Her head snapped around at the sharpness of my tone.

I went out into the night, feeling like a sullen, ungrateful girl. But why, if she'd had time to change into city clothes and put on make-up before leaving, couldn't she have found time to come and tell me?

Chapter Fifteen

Several times a week I received carefully crafted letters about weeds and gladioli and sparrows and such from a mum who never mentioned that she missed me. Obviously, she had loads of time on her hands.

Peter wrote encouraging letters that showed he'd looked up everything about the country but had no idea how it felt to live here. 'You should spend your leisure time safely by the pool,' he advised after I wrote about my mountainside rescue, 'since you're lucky enough to have the climate to enjoy it.' He didn't see that I was living like a hamster in a cage.

My best friend, Babs, was still my best friend, though she didn't write at all. And then she did. I ripped open the airmail envelope and sat on the bed to read her first letter to me since I got to Israel. It was postmarked 17 August. 'Dear Marlene,' it began. My own name looked odd to me, though Mum and Peter still used it.

Sorry I haven't written before.

She should be. I'd written to her six times.

I'm not much of a writer. I've also been very busy since Daddy made me ditch school at the end of the summer term, after my crummy exam results.

This was news!

Miss MacGrotty hauled me up in front of the class and told me I was a silly, silly, silly girl for leaving early and I'd never make anything of my life. I felt like asking her what she'd made of hers.

I laughed out loud at this. It struck me that it had been some time since I last laughed like that.

'People always need hairdressers,' Daddy said. I said I wanted to be a beautician, but it made no difference.

Mummy found me an apprenticeship at Coiffure, near the cathedral. Daddy says he'll set me up in my own salon when I'm qualified. Mummy will manage it, since I'm supposed to be such a birdbrain.

I don't like hairdressing, Marlene. My feet and back are agony by the end of the day, my hands are red and raw, and my lovely nails all broken.

The ladies can be so penny pinching. One last week tipped me a threepenny bit. I told her she should keep it since her need must be greater than mine.

I laughed again. She was outrageous.

I have training one evening a week and work every Saturday. It's all a bit much. Even so, I have to say I like it better than school. Everyone there seems childish to me now.

Babs had lost her freedom and her old friends. She was as fenced in as I was.

I have a new boyfriend, someone nearer to home than the cosh boy from Birmingham. He's more the sort you'd like, quite a dish really. I don't mind being seen out and about on his arm.

Lots of love, Babs x

I concluded, as she surely meant me to, that her new boyfriend was Peter. Babs' letter led to another sleepless night in my bed in Mutti's bungalow, where I would be staying more frequently now that my hours with the tinies had been slashed. I was starting school in Haifa.

Images of Peter crowded in. He was telling her things he'd told me, like the time during the war when a warden had left him and a friend in charge of a recreation ground, watching the skies for German parachutists who might attempt to land. He had a catapult and his friend had a sheath knife and they hoped to hold back the German army with that. Peter was laughing with her as we had laughed. He was cupping Babs' pretty face in his hands and kissing her ready lips as he never had mine. That left a big, lonely crater inside that wouldn't go away.

As the white light of morning finally seeped under the doorway, I turned over and said to Mutti, 'Come to England.'

She propped herself up on one elbow. 'I have no money. Last time, the kibbutz paid.'

'I'll get the money for you to come. I'll work when I get home and send it to you.'

She laughed her throaty laugh. 'But what would I do in England? There's nothing for me there.'

'There'd be me,' I said, knowing full well I wouldn't ever be enough for her.

'What would I do for a job? I hardly know the language.'

'That's not so. Your English is perfect.' I'd never considered this before. 'How did it get so good?'

'I had English in school.'

'I had French. It was one of my best subjects. But I can't speak it like you do English.'

'I used to read English books out loud to myself every night after you went to England. They weren't so easy to get; the Nazis had banned all kinds of books.'

This was quite a feat. I was impressed.

'I had to get good in case my little girl came back an English girl.'

'And I did.'

She nodded. 'And you did.'

A little bird was chirruping outside, welcoming the new day. Another, further away, joined in with a more melodic song. Together, they created a sweet harmony, though I was sure neither intended to be half of a duet.

'We must do what we must do.' Mutti lay back down again. 'I must stay in Israel with my own. And so must you.'

Chapter Sixteen

I got to wear the Mediterranean blue dress with the diamond at the bosom – not a real diamond, but a girl can dream – along with the white taffeta petticoat and the white sandals on a September Friday evening, a few weeks later. I had put up my hair and borrowed Mutti's white button earrings. I felt beautiful because the dress was beautiful, but also intensely shy because I was about to become the centre of attention.

I hid in the lavatory, as Dov had suggested I should, while the whole kibbutz came into the canteen for Shabbat supper. Our conversation was stilted. We had hardly spoken since Nazareth, but if he wasn't going to mention anything about it, neither was I.

When all the hustle and bustle died down, I slipped into the lobby and peered through the glass portholes of the double doors on my tiptoes.

Dov was standing between the serving hatches of the separate meat and dairy kitchens, addressing the assembled kibbutzniks. He had on a clean white shirt and wore a white skullcap on his head. Beside him was the small Sabbath table covered with a white tablecloth. On it were a flacon of red wine, a silver chalice, a silver candlestick bearing two ivory candles, and a silver platter, which you couldn't see because it was under a cloth that hid two giant loaves of sweet *challah* bread, made with eggs and olive oil.

Behind me, there was a tawny glow in the sky. The grass was turning black-green outside now that the sun had dropped from sight. I wished *I* could drop from sight. A whole herd of elephants was having a water fight in the mudhole of my belly.

'... I give you... our Lena!' Dov finished in Hebrew, raising his voice and a hand in my direction.

I came in to rhythmic clapping, with my mouth in a fixed smile to mask my terror.

'*Nu*, Lena,' Dov said, after I had joined him at the front and everyone had quietened down. 'Now you are Israeli!'

The enthusiastic shouts, applause, and Middle Eastern gurgling sound they call ululation swelled as he held up my Israeli ID and said, 'Here is your *Teudat Zehut*.'

We had finally provided the authorities with all the paperwork and photos they needed. The interview, at the end of August, had been partly in my halting Hebrew with Dov and Mutti chipping in, and partly in the government operative's bad English.

Dov handed the ID to me. 'How do you feel, Lena?'

I couldn't begin to tell these people how I felt in English, let alone in Hebrew. A picture popped into my head of a surfer riding a giant wave. I had gone along with the things put in place for me without pausing to consider my options. And now there was no turning back.

But the room was expectant. I had to say something, I realised. '*Mahgishah metzuyan*,' I said – I feel wonderful. It made them happy. They clapped and called out some more.

Everyone stood as someone began to play *Hatikvah,* the national anthem, on a clarinet. I had learned the words and was able to sing along.

To all the European Holocaust survivors in the room, to all the Middle Eastern Jews whose nations turned against them and expelled them when the State of Israel was created, the song's message of freedom shone like a sparkling gemstone.

I had never not been free, or at least couldn't remember ever not being free. And I barely recognised myself as a Jew. But with all my heart I embraced the dream that was becoming reality here, a Jewish homeland, after 2,000 years of exile. It was a mystery to me how I could feel so patriotic about Israel and miss England at the same time.

Because miss England I did, and not just because of Peter. I missed the soft green countryside and the quaint streets of Canterbury with its Tudor, Georgian, Victorian and 1930s houses, sometimes all in a row. I missed the ancient cathedral with its tall tower, visible from afar in the bottom of the teacup shape that constituted the city. I missed the gentleness of the climate and of the people.

Dov invited me to light the candles. As I placed my hands over my eyes, he encouraged all the women to say the blessing along with me, for which I was grateful as I was still hesitant with the words. Together, we thanked God for sanctifying us through His commandment to light the Sabbath lights.

I was the first, after Dov, to sip from the chalice of wine he blessed. And the first to eat a piece of the *challah* bread he broke after blessing it.

As the bread and wine were passed around, Yaacov walked in, playing the fiddle. The clarinet player joined him in a lively tune that turned the room wild. People from every table jumped to their feet to converge on Dov and me, clapping their hands in time to the music.

Sara, my willowy supervisor, normally so offhand, pressed forward to congratulate me. People I didn't know told me, '*Baruch habaah*'– welcome – and *mazal tov.*

As I was scanning the crowd for Mutti, she strode in, wearing her slinky black dress and singing *Hava Nagila*. On her wrist was Oma's bracelet.

I was tugged into a circle of enthusiastic Israeli dancing.

Later that evening, I paused to stare at myself in the mirror of the ladies' lavatory as I washed my hands. I looked like a chip off the old block. I really did. The dark-haired, dark-eyed, cherry-red-lipped young woman looking back at me might have been Mutti herself, the way she would have been as I watched her from the wings of the Bremen theatre.

As I stood looking at myself, something stirred deep within me that swelled in my throat and brought tears close to the surface. For the first time, the fairy tale of my early years that explained and justified how I came to be here tonight felt more than just words on a slip of paper supplied by the Central British Fund for Relief and Rehabilitation. Could I really go the whole hog, I wondered, and turn back into the person I had started out as?

That week, we had celebrated Rosh Hashanah, Jewish New Year. We had dipped apples in honey and eaten them, to make the new year sweet. That week, I had officially become Lena Levi, an Israeli citizen. There could not have been a better moment for new beginnings. So why were my heartstrings being tugged in a thousand different directions?

Mutti breezed in. I quickly swallowed my agitation and sent her a broad smile. We grinned at one another in the mirror as she touched up her lipstick. Oma's diamonds flashed rainbow sparkles at her wrist.

'Just give it time, Lena. I didn't feel like I belonged here at first.' She spoke as if she knew what was going on with me.

Strains of lively *klezmer* music came from the canteen. The music was Ashkenazi, from Eastern Europe, with clarinet, accordion and flute. Yaacov was playing the fiddle. He wasn't Ashkenazi. He was a Middle Eastern Jew from Iran, a Sephardi. Whenever I overheard him playing in his bungalow his lilting melodies sounded like the sort that belly dancers might wiggle their hips to. But he'd adapted and mixed in.

'Bremen is a big business city,' Mutti said, 'with grand buildings either side of the River Weser. The winters are cold, the summers are not too hot, and the streets are clean enough to eat off.'

The fond gleam of nostalgia in her eyes amazed me. How could she feel that way after everything Germany had done to her?

She slipped her lipstick back into her clutch bag, gave a little wave, and clapped herself out of the door, heading for the canteen where I could hear everyone clapping along to the music. They were all a long way from where they had started out and trying to make the best of it. The difference between them and me was they had nowhere else to go.

Outside, the night was silky warm. The moon and stars twinkled in the domed black sky above while lizards posed on the path. An insect orchestra was playing along with the band inside. Two shadowy figures were sitting close to one another on the bench, across in the children's play area.

Mutti came up behind me. 'Why are you standing like a statue in the middle of the square?'

I nodded towards the silhouetted figures. 'Is that…'

Mutti followed my gaze. 'Yes, Dov and Sara. I could see that coming.'

I couldn't. I had no clue.

'It is sad that his pain has left him unfeeling.'

Unfeeling would not have been how I'd have described Dov.

'It's the same for me – sadly.'

Was that why she craved drama? To feel something?

'He had a wife.'

'Did she die?' Something in Mutti's tone made me think that.

She nodded. 'Her name was Miri. I saw photographs. She was very beautiful. They were in a convoy.'

'You don't have to tell me.' I didn't want to hear.

'They were in a convoy at Bab el Wad. It's a valley, just outside…'

'I know about Bab el Wad. Remember the song?'

'He was in a jeep behind her truck. One moment she was blowing kisses out the back curtain. The next… gone. Everyone in the truck. A grenade.'

It was small wonder that Dov had turned in on himself after such a tragedy. I felt sad for him – and guilty. If I'd known, I'd have been nicer.

'He told you all this, Mutti?' I hadn't realised they were that close.

'Ach! How do you say – pillow talk.'

My jaw dropped.

She laughed, enjoying my shocked reaction.

I didn't want to know about her lovers. I was the product of one of them, which was not a very nice thought.

She lit a cigarette. Her and her death sticks. It glowed as she inhaled deeply. She didn't seem to care that she was setting her insides on fire.

'We couldn't connect,' she said. 'Sara's solid. She'll be good for him.'

I'd had enough of this conversation. 'I'm going to bed.'

'I also was thinking about turning in.' She stared at Dov and Sara as she dragged on her cigarette. 'But, then' – she blew out a cloud of smoke and winked at me – 'the night is young!'

With a skip in her step, she turned back towards the canteen.

My new sandals had left four little blister bubbles on the tops of my toes. I rubbed them and then I rubbed my earlobes. Mutti's earrings had pinched. I hung my beautiful blue dress and petticoat in Mutti's wardrobe and put on the summer pyjamas Mum had sent me: a loose top and striped shorts in peach-and-biscuit-coloured cotton with a thin gold stripe between. She'd sewn them herself.

I could see her in the back room at home, leaning in towards the little light above the fabric she was feeding through her sewing machine as it whirred. Outside, clouds of battleship grey scudded past as the wind tossed the weeping willow's tendrils. All that was a world away.

It was funny to think that in England I would have thought the fabric exotic, the stuff of a king's costume in a nativity play. Yet here, the pattern looked quintessentially English to me.

Such a lovely word, I thought: quintessential.

I draped my hair around my shoulders, pouting at myself in the narrow mirror. No matter how I tried to brush out the kinks from my updo, they remained. I should have been happy. My hair was usually dead straight, which was so unfashionable.

What an odd creature I was! Just a short while before, I'd told everyone I felt *metzuyan*. Now my spirits were on a slippery slope and I didn't know why. Part of it was surely that I couldn't shake off the feeling that I was an imposter, even though I wasn't. My paperwork confirmed that. My *Teudat Zehut* was a blue booklet, printed in Hebrew and Arabic, that opened at the back and read from right to left.

I looked down at my pyjamas. The pleasure I got from wearing them seemed somehow tainted by the fact that I was living out the destiny of the little Jewess from Bremen. My enjoyment felt sneaky, disloyal, ungrateful. I flung myself on the bed. Why did everything have to be so complex?

'You're wrong,' a voice said in my head. 'It's as simple as can be: she had no destiny.'

That was true. The little Jewess would surely have died if she'd remained in Germany. But she didn't. And somewhere, in the terror of crossing the North Sea or crying herself to sleep in Wales, she got rubbed out. Either way, she died.

The girl who had scowled back at me from Mutti's mirror was the changeling who took her place. That girl liked plain food, milk in her tea, picnics and country walks. She liked learning about the Tudor kings and queens. She even liked algebra. She liked all the things I liked.

Chapter Seventeen

The next morning at breakfast, one of the nursery assistants said Sara wanted to see me. My footsteps echoed through the empty nursery building as I went up the stairs. Practically all the children were with their parents and the rest had already been taken across to the pool. I intended to take Mutti's advice and spend my day off by the pool too.

'So, go get a tan. Swim with your friends,' she said when she finally came to bed at daybreak and announced that she had guard duty that day, up on the mountain.

There was nothing else to do.

Sara looked stern as I entered her office. That didn't faze me. It was her usual way.

'I have learned that you're a Nazarene,' she said, before my backside had quite reached the visitor's chair. That was what they called Christians here. My stomach flipped, like I'd been found out for something bad – which, of course, I hadn't.

'Is it true?'

Dov must have told her. That didn't seem fair. I hadn't told anyone about his violent outburst.

I put on my defiant face. 'Yes.'

'You must not speak of this to the children.'

I resented the bars she was adding to my prison. 'Why not?'

'The parents would not like it.' I must have looked sceptical, for she added, 'You would not welcome a Jew teaching the little children in England that the Messiah never came. Would you?'

I supposed not. I found myself reassuring her. 'I haven't spoken of it so far.'

I felt bad the moment I said that because I knew that Jesus told us to tell everybody about Him.

'You must promise me that you will not, or you won't be able to continue.'

I wanted desperately to fit in. So, I promised.

I lay on my towel on the grass by the pool in my black regulation swimming costume, with my thoughts all over the place. I didn't feel like I fitted in at the school, which I'd started going to three weeks before. I was just one more tiresome foreigner to be talked at slowly in simple terms, like I was a bit dim. I got myself sent to see the principal in Jewish Studies class after protesting to Miss van Gelder when she said, 'In this class, we are establishing historical occupation of the Land. God is irrelevant.'

She was talking nonsense, using God's words as proof and then saying He had nothing to do with any of it. I told her so. Sara's rules, Mutti telling me to 'give it time' and the argument in Nazareth with Dov were all jumbled up together and going around in my head, along with Miss van Gelder's words. Those of Babs in her letter too – perhaps hers more than anyone's.

I'd taken a dip earlier and wanted to swim again, but the pool was too crowded now. There was nowhere to get out of the sun. The tinies with my colleagues from the nursery had taken all the shade under the covered area. I was burning up.

All around me, families were jabbering in Hebrew. Last night, everyone had gathered around to congratulate me on becoming Israeli. This morning, they were making me feel like an outsider again. On top of that, I had to mind my Ps & Qs and not speak of what I believed in.

It was too hot and too lonely here. I gathered up my things. It would be stifling in Mutti's bungalow, but at least my isolation would not be so obvious.

I was surprised to hear laughter as I opened the door. Mutti was home after all.

This gave me a boost as I sailed in. 'So, you're not working today, Daddy-O?'

The room was gloomy and strangely still, hung with swirls of cigarette smoke. The shutters were closed. I screwed up my eyes. At first it was hard to make out what I was seeing.

Mutti was sitting on her bed, holding an overflowing ashtray and grinning broadly at me, like a gargoyle. A man was sitting right beside her with his shirt unbuttoned. As his face in the shadows took form, I saw that he was smiling too.

'Shalom, Lena,' Dov said. 'How are you?' His smile wasn't nice, more gloating.

'What is this?' I cried, as if I didn't know. Everything in me was screaming to storm straight back out of the door, but I clung to the forlorn hope that this might be some terrible misunderstanding. I wrapped my arms around my body and held on tight.

As the silence grew heavy with betrayal, I realised that the conclusion I'd jumped to was right on the money. 'Some guard duty!'

'I didn't think you'd be back so soon, Lena,' Mutti said.

'Clearly!'

She'd planned this and had said any old thing just to get rid of me.

Yet it was Dov I rounded on, eyes flaring, even as they brimmed with tears. 'What about Sara?'

He was taken aback. 'Sara? Why do you ask about her?'

'I think she loves you.'

His laughter was a sneer. 'You don't care about Sara.'

I cared that they had secrets from her, that they were laughing at her behind her back, that they thought only of themselves. But I would be wasting my breath to tell them so.

The stench of their cigarettes layering itself over the smell of chlorine on my skin was making me feel sick. *They* were making me feel sick. My hand trembled as I reached for the door handle and went out. There seemed nowhere to go. So, I walked the perimeter fence, torturing myself with memories of the Saturdays I'd left behind – lingering breakfasts, wanders through cool, wet woods, and hunts for buried treasure on the shelves of the public library.

When I got so hot that I was starting to sway, I made my way to the nursery building, where I held on to the handrail as I dragged myself up the stairs to my bed at the end of the tinies' dorm. There, head pounding, I flung myself down. I threw my arm that smelled of my swim across my face and chewed on its soft flesh.

I'd take a shower, I decided. As soon as my legs were my own again, I would wash it all away.

'Have you seen Dov?' Sara's head was poked around the curtains of my cubicle. Her expression was pleasant, as if my talking-to this morning had never been. 'I'm looking for Dov. Have you seen him?'

Now was my chance to get my own back. But after only the briefest of hesitations, I shook my head. I couldn't wilfully hurt her.

'If you see him, tell him I'm looking for him,' she called back, already halfway down the corridor.

'Alright,' I said, though she probably didn't hear me.

I'd lied, but for good reason – to avoid causing her pain. My arm went back over my eyes. I began thinking of Mum, who didn't tell me the truth because she wanted to spare me pain. I hadn't understood how she, who loved truth, could do that. Now I did.

Chapter Eighteen

Kibbutz Eshkadosh
Israel

21st September 1950

Dear Mum,

Today is Yom Kippur, the Jewish festival for asking for forgiveness of our sins. Prayers and communal confession went on into the night yesterday and have been continuing all day today in the canteen.

The whole country is deathly quiet. I'm writing this letter in a whisper, sitting on the porch outside Mutti's bungalow, while she takes a nap inside.

It's not so hard to fast, but I do have a headache. We don't even take a drink for twenty-five hours.

I realised with an abrupt rush of heat that I was probably guilty of breaking the rules yet again – rules that most of the kibbutzniks at Kibbutz Eshkadosh followed, regardless of the fact they were secular. For surely I shouldn't be doing any work on this Sabbath of Sabbaths. And didn't writing a letter constitute work?

Luckily, no one seemed to have seen me. Though a few parents were over in the nursery playground with their children, the lawn of the quadrangle before me was deserted. With its well-watered grass of vivid green, and cactus flowers and poppies around the edge, it looked lovely, particularly in contrast to the dusty slopes and trees that lay beyond the kibbutz. We'd seen no rain since I got here. There'd be none until November, they said.

Yom Kippur was full of spaces to look back. I was feeling wistful for expeditions to quaint churches in chocolate-box villages surrounding Canterbury and the ancient pilgrim pathways that led to them, across pastures of sheep and through fields of wheat, by ancient woodlands where, even at fourteen and three quarters, I might make believe I was Robin Hood, if no one was watching.

I'd also been going over in my mind how I came to be here, and couldn't quite work out what had happened. I remembered my fear that if I let Mutti go, then my hidden identity that was only just beginning to unravel would be lost. I was focused on who I once was when, perhaps, I should have paid more attention to the direction in which I was flinging myself.

Groans came from inside the bungalow, followed by whimpers that sounded like a dog in distress. These sounds were followed by thrashing about and cries: *'Nein, nein, nein!'*

Mutti was having another nightmare. I went to her. Sweat was beading on her upper lip. Her body was twitching.

'It's alright, Mutti.' I bent to touch her shoulder. 'You're safe.' She opened unseeing eyes. Her breath smelled stale. No doubt mine did too. Our bellies were empty.

'You were having a dream.'

'*Ja*?' Her gaze was bewildered. She was still half in the nightmare. She shifted to let me sit beside her on the narrow bed. She held my hand between hers. They were hot and damp.

'It was so strange.' She licked her lips. 'I was in the Rambam, giving birth to you. When they cut the cord and took you away, it felt so lonely, here.' She laid a hand across her belly. I nodded. I knew how it felt to have a cord cut.

'I wanted to cry. I thought they wouldn't bring you back.'

I pushed back the strands of hair sticking to her brow. 'What's the Rambam?'

'It's the big hospital, here in Haifa.' She shook her head. 'It makes no sense. You weren't born here.'

She clambered out of bed and headed unsteadily for the table. 'I need a cigarette.'

She put one in her mouth, then swore in German as she fumbled to light it. 'It's Yom Kippur. I can't smoke.' She put the cigarette back. A fit of coughing followed.

'You shouldn't smoke, Mutti.'

'Imma.' She returned to sit on the bed beside me.

She was wearing a white lawn nightdress she'd bought during her spree in Tel Aviv. It had a bodice of Calais lace. She lived like a kid in a sweet shop. Every chance she got, she reached for whatever shiny wrapper offered the next sugar rush. That was what had happened with Dov, no doubt, who I'd seen earlier, holding hands with Sara. Clearly, their relationship was still going strong.

'I remember now. Everything in the dream suddenly shifted. I was standing on the quay in Bremen, beside the ship that would take you to England. I looked and looked, but I couldn't see you. You must have been inside.'

'I expect.' I stroked her shoulder, over and over.

'I watched them untie the big ropes, ready to leave.' She screwed up her face. 'I had the same ache inside as when they cut the cord. It was like a bit of me was cut off. The ship got smaller and smaller, until it was just a little dot on the horizon. As I watched, I had that same emptiness, in here.' She tapped her belly again.

'That was only your dream.' Underneath my soft tone, I was rattled that she'd rewritten history. 'That's not how it really was.'

Her eyebrows shot up. 'I saw your ship go.'

'It's one of the few things I remember. You said goodbye and walked away.'

'I don't think so.' She laid a hand over her eyes, like she was rerunning the memory through in her mind. 'No, I stayed and watched, I'm sure. Until I couldn't see you any more.'

I had said what I had to say. There was nothing to add. After a moment, she said, 'I think that's how it was... It's not so important.'

It was important to me.

'What time is it?' she said.

'About four, I think.'

'In the afternoon?'

'Yes.'

Did she really think it might be four in the morning? She got back into bed and closed her eyes. 'Wake me up at five-thirty. I must go for the closing prayers for the dead.'

I got to my feet. 'You won't leave. Will you?' she said.

'I'll be right here, just outside the door.'

'That's not what I meant.' Her voice was drowsy.

I returned to the porch and took up my pen. Doubts overtook my certainty. I was three years old when Mutti said goodbye and walked away. Even if I didn't remember seeing her after that, she might still have been there.

I finished my letter to Mum:

> *I was wondering what Jesus did on Yom Kippur when He was on earth, since He was perfect and wouldn't have needed to confess his sins. However, He was a Jew who respected the Old Testament rules. So, I expect He kept it and fasted. He became like a forever Yom Kippur when He took all our sins on Himself when He was crucified.*

Thinking about all this at the service this morning had left me unsure whether I should stand up with everyone else today and ask for forgiveness, but I did anyway. I thought about the sort of person I'd been over the last year and said sorry to God.

> *I realised that I haven't been very nice to you, Mum, especially just before I left. I'm sorry that I didn't appreciate all you've done for me. And I'm sorry I didn't tell you before now that I miss you, because I do. A lot.*
>
> *I had to write this now and tell you.*

Please write back soon, and not about pruning the rose bushes.

With love from your daughter,

Marlene

xxx

Chapter Nineteen

Mum's reply, which came after a couple of weeks, was under my pillow. It didn't say a whole lot, but I clung to what it did say.

> *I'm sorry you don't want to hear about the garden any more!*
> *You don't need to apologise for anything.*
> *With much love,*
> *Mum*

I had no good reason to want to go. Everyone in England was forgetting me. And yet I wanted to go.

Leave.

That night, in the middle of the night, I reached across and gave Mutti a shake and told her.

'You can't go,' she said, as we both blinked in the dazzle of the light she'd flicked on. 'Everyone goes through this. It will pass.' She frowned at me. 'Anyway, I decide what you do until you're twenty-one. And I say no.'

I thought that was a bit rich! She hadn't made a single decision about anything in my upbringing. Even here in

Israel. Dov and Sara had been better mentors to me than she had.

'I'll be old enough, at sixteen, to go in the army to fight and die for this country, so I think I'm capable of knowing where I want to live.'

'Surely you want to stay with me?' She looked wounded. 'I've lost everybody else.'

I felt bad about that. Nevertheless, I said what had to be said. 'I hardly know you.'

That was the truth. I didn't know her any better now than at the end of that first week in England. She wasn't a woman anyone could know. She had all the appearance of wearing her heart on her sleeve but all the closed-up secrecy of someone too damaged to have one.

But she was looking so hurt that I hedged. 'Maybe I'll come back.'

She turned her head away. 'You never would.'

'But you can't keep me here. I don't belong.'

'None of us belongs. All we share is a dream.'

'That's just it.' A lump swelled in my throat. I had never undergone prejudice or persecution except here as a Christian, and that was nothing compared to what most of my fellow kibbutzniks had suffered. 'It's not a dream I ever needed before.'

'You'll get used to things here eventually.'

'I want to live without barbed wire and high fences. I want to walk in the fields again.' I wanted my life back, even if Peter was lost to me.

Silence.

'I miss my mum.'

Long silence.

She chewed on her lip. 'You're my little girl, Lena. I love you.'

I didn't believe her capable of love. And I couldn't say I loved her back. All I had for her was compassion.

Abruptly, she changed tack. 'You can't go, anyway.' Her voice was bright. 'We have no money.'

'You have the money Mum gave you in case. Now is in case.'

She opened her palms. 'All gone.'

'All gone?' A buzzing set up in my brain. 'How?'

'On expenses.'

I narrowed my eyes. 'New clothes and things from Tel Aviv?'

She grinned, looking both sheepish and impish.

'All of it?'

I had to hear her say it, so I'd be absolutely sure I'd got it straight.

'Yes, all of it.'

She had sacrificed my safety net for her giddy moment of extravagance.

'What will I do?' I was too stunned even to be angry.

Her smile now was full of sickly charm. 'Stay?'

The days that followed were horrible. Mutti had betrayed me and school was challenging. Everyone there ignored me with the exception of a new boy from Romania who, discovering my Christian Bible on my desk after the Jewish Studies lesson, made a pantomime of picking it up as if it burned his fingers, and launched it out of the window.

I went down, picked it up off the pavement, dusted it down and hugged it to me. That was when I decided not to go back inside. In my pocket, I had the card of the rabbi I had met on the ship that brought me here. I'd been carrying it around with me ever since my midnight conversation with Mutti about leaving, three days earlier.

I could read the address now, which was Bat Galim, an area of Haifa down near the sea. The port was that way too. I hadn't been there since my arrival back in June. We were into October now.

I made my way downhill, past shoppers and stray cats that draped themselves from roofs and across dustbins. The weather was gradually getting cooler. It was pleasant, like a warm summer's day in England.

A passenger ship had just docked as I came to the port. A lot of calling and waving was going on between the passengers up high on the deck and the crowds gathered below to meet them. I joined them, standing a little apart, off to the side.

The expectant faces took me back to the excitement I'd felt upon my arrival in Israel. I thought I had come to Paradise. Clearly, these droves of new immigrants thought so too.

All that seemed a lot longer than four months ago. I had been a different person then, stepping into my identity as Lena Levi, or so I thought. Now I was full of her, but Marlene wouldn't move over and make room. So, it was quite a squeeze and the chatter going on in my head between them was driving me doolally. For, seemingly, both wanted to be in charge.

Port workers slid the gangway across and people began to disembark. There were tears and all the emotional reunions that went on when my ship docked. It was better entertainment than an afternoon at the pictures. One or two bowed to kiss the ground and raise their hands to heaven, home at last. They didn't know what real life was like here.

Disembarkation was temporarily halted by the arrival of a Magen David Adom ambulance – the Israeli equivalent of the Red Cross – a long, low, American-style vehicle that looked like a white hearse. It had a strident siren and a flashing light that blazed on as it inched its way through the crowds on the quay.

Once past them, it picked up speed before pulling up abruptly at the far end of the dock, alongside a shabby cargo vessel flying a red flag with a Union Jack in the corner. It was a flag I'd learned at Girl Guides: the British Merchant Navy.

Two ambulancemen ran up the gangplank with a stretcher, only to emerge, moments later, carrying a patient who seemed to be writhing in agony. They were followed by a ship's officer, dressed in white, and a second man, in white overalls – the cook, judging by his belly. I watched, curious, as they loaded the patient into the ambulance. I supposed him to be a member of the crew and therefore potentially British.

The ambulance turned around and came past us again, light flashing, siren blaring, and sped into the road.

I expected to hear it wailing into the distance. But that didn't happen. The hospital was right there, beyond an assortment of docked Israeli naval craft – a long white building hugging the shore, four or five storeys high.

I lost all interest in visiting the rabbi. The wheels of my brain were turning as a plan took shape in my head.

Chapter Twenty

The following day, I returned to the port after school. I tried to reach the merchant ship with the British flag, but the officials at the port entrance barrier wouldn't let me pass. Being a resourceful sort of a person, I didn't just give up. I headed for the hospital. It turned out to be the Rambam hospital that Mutti had dreamt about. I found out later that it was named after a famous medieval Jewish philosopher from Spain called Maimonides. How they came to call him Rambam was anybody's guess.

It certainly was a busy place. Even so, it wasn't too hard to find the British patient who'd arrived by ambulance from a British merchant ship twenty-four hours earlier. It was the first time I could remember that speaking hesitant Hebrew with an English accent worked in my favour.

Of course, I didn't know for sure the patient would be British, but it turned out he was. His name was Patrick Harrison. He was a fresh-faced boy of sixteen from West Ham in London. He worked in the ship's kitchen, which he called the galley. He had undergone an emergency appendix operation and was recovering well.

He shunted himself up in bed, wincing but perky, as I approached. He made it plain that he was very happy to see the friendly face of an English-speaking visitor, very pleased to have someone able to ask the nurses questions in Hebrew on his behalf.

His ship, the MS *Trevor*, would be departing without him that night, he told me in his Cockney accent. The ship's agent would be sorting out his passage home as soon as he was well again.

'I thought you was her, when you first come up,' he said, with a grin. 'I couldn't believe me luck. You're awful pretty.'

I didn't feel the same way about him. There were more freckles than boy. He even had freckles on his eyelids. He was more than a year older than me, already in the world of work and well-travelled. Yet, he seemed like a young boy. I'd done a lot of growing up in Israel, I realised.

I couldn't believe my luck when the captain in white uniform and the big-bellied man in white overalls, who was indeed the cook, arrived for a visit. We soon had my working passage home as replacement galley-hand arranged. I would be departing Haifa on the MS *Trevor*, bound for Southampton, England, tonight at ten.

I headed outside in a daze. What I was about to do was huger by far than anything I'd ever done before. My impulsive decision to come to Israel with Mutti seemed effortless by comparison.

I was going home of my own free will. I was grasping my future in my hands. I couldn't believe it was happening. Was I doing the right thing? That was the big question. I hadn't considered Mutti. Now that I was about to leave, it struck me how much I'd miss her, not to mention that Israel was a beautiful country I'd hardly seen anything of yet. Had I been too hasty? Shouldn't I think this through a bit?

As I crossed the road to the bus stop, excitement was making me tingly, but it was mixed with daggers of fear and hollow dread. There were some difficult things I needed to do, and I was terrified they'd go wrong and spoil everything. I needed to get back to Kibbutz Eshkadosh for my passport and a few other things, like the Mediterranean blue dress. Then I would have to tell Mutti, which was going to be terrible. Finally, I needed to get myself back here for tonight's sailing of the *Trevor*.

There was no need to worry, I told myself. I had loads of time. And Haifa buses were reliable, although this area of Bat Galim – which means Daughter of the Waves – was unfamiliar to me. I was looking hard at the schedules to find a bus that would take me across town to connect with the one I usually took home from school.

At my back was the inevitable building site, one of the many developments of plain apartment blocks going up everywhere to house new immigrants. There'd be no peace from the port traffic and constant ambulance sirens for anyone who moved in here.

An ambulance was coming now – a crescendo of wailing to make you want to plug your ears. It rounded the corner from the main road and swung into the hospital driveway. Clearly, the rush was on to save some poor blighter's life.

As I waited at the bus stop, a khaki jeep with a canvas canopy appeared, trailing smoke. It looked just like the one from the kibbutz. In fact, it *was* the one from the kibbutz, with Dov at the wheel and Sara beside him. Oh dear! I hoped they weren't looking for me. But that was impossible. There wasn't anywhere I was supposed to be between school home time and supper. So, I wasn't missing. Not yet.

The jeep turned into the hospital driveway and came to a halt, puffing black smoke signals from the exhaust. I could see Sara in silhouette, turning around and pointing. She'd spotted me. She got out of the jeep and came towards the road. 'Lena, this way!' She beckoned me to cross the rush-hour traffic. As soon as a gap came in the cars, bicycles, buses, trucks, horses, mules and donkeys, I darted across the road to join her.

To my surprise, she motioned for me to sit in the front, next to Dov, while she jumped in the back behind him. He pulled away, but we only drove thirty yards or so, to the car park. He cut the engine and turned to me. 'How did you hear?'

I looked at him blankly.

'Have you been inside?' he asked. 'How are things looking?'

'Things?'

'Can they operate?'

He must mean Patrick. I had no idea how they'd discovered my plans.

'They already did,' I said.

His eyebrows shot up. 'What? The ambulance only just arrived at the hospital.'

I was totally confused. 'What are we talking about?'

Sara leaned forward. 'Your mother.'

Sara's words sent me reeling as I processed them. 'My mother? Is she alright?' Fear surged through me. 'What happened?'

She frowned. 'You didn't know she was shot?'

'You mean Mutti?' For a second, as I'd tried to piece together what was happening, I thought they'd come looking for me with awful news about Mum. 'Where was she shot?'

Dov slammed his hands down on the steering wheel, frustrated. 'At the top of the mountain.'

'I mean, where was she hit?'

He opened his door. 'Come on. We need to find her.' The three of us scrambled out and hurried towards Casualty.

'Who shot her?' I asked. 'Will she be alright?'

'In the head,' Sara said. 'She was shot in the head.'

It was weird, like I'd already lived through this bit of my life, like I already knew.

It was touch and go whether she'd pull through, they said. Even if she survived the operation, Mutti might be deaf on one side. She might have brain damage. She might never walk again. We were brought into a side room, barely bigger than a cupboard, to wait. We sat. Dov and Sara were opposite me, holding hands.

The window looked out over the sea, which had taken on a purple sheen as the sun descended. I had a skewed view of the port. The lights were going on out there, on the quay and on the ships, glowing as the skies began to darken.

'Sweet Jesus,' I prayed in my head, 'I beg you, please spare Mutti's life. Make the surgery work. Make it so she has no brain damage. Restore her to full health, please. Be with the surgeon. Help him work fast. Do it now, so I can still board the ship tonight and work my passage to England. Please, please, please. Amen.'

I knew I was supposed to talk as if the blessing had already been given and thank Him for His intervention, but I lacked the faith to do it.

As we waited, it grew properly dark outside.

I could still slip away, go through the door, say I was going to the lavatory, and do what I had planned to do – get my passport, return to the *Trevor*.

I need not say any goodbyes. I need never see any of them again.

Israel was too dangerous. You could get picked off by some trigger-happy sniper who didn't know you from Adam but wanted to kill you anyway. Even if you were only keeping cattle.

'I could still go now,' I told myself.

Dov brought us coffees and egg sandwiches. I drank my coffee but couldn't eat.

The operation was taking a long time.

If they came now and told us all would be well, I could still make my ship.

I ran through memories of Mutti like a funny movie:

... looking beautiful in her cherry-red top and matching lipstick as she picked her way down the stairs towards me in her high heels.

... pulling a crab-apple face at the pickle in her sandwich.

… strutting up and down in the bungalow, belting out her patriotic *Bab el Wad* song to cheer me up.

… breezing in with bags and bags of stuff, like we were millionaires.

… singing *Hava Nagila* to me in my blue dress with the taffeta petticoat, in front of the whole kibbutz.

… calling back at me, 'The night is young!' as if she hadn't a care in all the world.

The surgeon, a big, hairy man of about forty-five, came in wearing his gown. Black hair was sprouting from the base of his neck, along his arms, and even tufty in his ears, though he was mostly bald on top. 'I am Dr Rosenblum. You are the daughter of Rochel Levi?'

'I am.'

He sat down next to me like a deflating balloon, as if he was all in. 'She lives.'

Dov, Sara and I exchanged tentative smiles.

'It is too early to predict her outlook. She has survived the surgery, but we cannot tell the extent of damage to her brain. Of course, the best outcome would be that there is none. Only time will tell.'

He laid his bunch-of-banana, hairy fingers on his knees. 'She is still very unwell.' He stared out of the window. His nails were very short and pink, his knuckles red and scrubbed, with only the odd straggly hair on them. 'I have to tell you that she may not make it.'

He sounded so sad, I had to comfort him. 'Don't worry, doctor. You're trying your best.'

'It's all we can do.' He whistled through his teeth as he got to his feet. 'All we can do.'

'Thank you.'

Sara and Dov echoed me.

'Can I see her?'

'Just you. And for a couple of minutes only. She needs complete rest. Come, I will tell the nurse.'

I followed him out.

Strong smells of iodine and cleaning fluid hit me as I tiptoed in. The smells were doing battle with Mutti's potpourri perfume, which was winning. This made me smile in spite of all. One way or another, she would always make her presence felt.

Seeing her was a shock. She looked tiny in the big bed in the semi-darkness, with just one powerful light shining on her head, which looked huge since it was bandaged. She was lying scarily still. But I could hear a metronome-like ticking coming from somewhere. Surely that was a machine measuring her heartbeat. A good sign? I made myself step closer. What I could see of her face was as pale as the pillow.

They had her rigged up with all kinds of tubes. An inverted bottle above her head was connected to a needle that went into her left hand. Another snaked up from an oxygen canister on the floor to a mask that covered her mouth and nose. Yet another, coming from the foot of the bed, led to a big bottle with an inch or two of urine in it.

It was only 8pm. There would still be time to make my sailing if I left soon. I clung to the idea of doing that, though there was a heavy feeling inside of me that my lovely plans were turning to make-believe. It wasn't this that made me bang my head against the wall, however. I was enraged that some person had set out to murder such a beautiful, vivacious bundle of dynamite as my Mutti.

Chapter Twenty-one

'How is your mother?' was Inspector Neuberger's icebreaker question.

I shrugged. I was sure he knew better than I did how she was.

He was a tall man in his fifties with long hands and feet, a beaked nose and wispy hair. I thought he must have lost a lot of weight, for his dark suit hung on him like on a coat hanger. But maybe he'd got it from a jumble sale.

He was sitting in the waiting room, when I came out from seeing Mutti. Two uniformed police officers who came with him were outside, by the nurses' station. He handed me his card as he introduced himself and asked me if I would answer some questions. Then he asked Sara and Dov to step outside, leaving the two of us alone.

I wasn't nervous. I had read a lot of Agatha Christie detective novels and knew what to expect. 'Will you be able to solve this?' I asked. 'Will you catch him?'

'By the end of our investigation, we will know everything,' he said, with a slow smile. He sounded pretty sure of himself, which was a good thing. He tugged a blue silk handkerchief from his pocket, as if he were going to do a magic trick. Instead, he proceeded to blow his nose, noisily and at length. When he was satisfied he had all the snot gone, he tucked it away again in his trouser pocket.

He took a notebook and pencil from his breast pocket. Poised to write, he looked up. 'Where were you today, between two and four?'

'Me?'

He nodded encouragingly.

I frowned. 'Am I a suspect?'

'Should you be?'

I wondered why I felt uncomfortable. I had nothing to hide. 'Well, after school, I came here, to the hospital.'

He wrote it down. 'Why?'

'Why?'

'Yes. Why?'

'I was visiting someone.'

'I see.' He made a note. 'Who?'

I shifted in my chair. 'His name is Patrick Harrison.' Golly! I really hadn't wanted all this to come out.

'Patrick Ha-rri-son,' he repeated, writing it down as I spelled it for him. 'Is he a friend?'

'No.'

He looked puzzled.

'More of an acquaintance.'

'So, how do you know one another? Does Patrick Harrison go to school with you?'

'No, his home is in England.'

'So, you know him from England?'

'Not really, no.' I cleared my throat. 'Actually, I met him here. He works on one of the ships in the port.'

The inspector looked surprised. 'He is your boyfriend?'

'Not at all!' I didn't much like the suggestion that I picked up sailors off the boats. 'If you must know, he has just had his appendix out.'

I waited while Inspector Neuberger again took out his blue silk handkerchief and gave it a wave. This signalled another lengthy nose blow and snot hunt.

'Do you have a cold?'

'Allergies.' He tucked it into his pocket again. 'Now,' he said, as if we were starting over. 'I am having difficulty understanding how you came to know this Patrick Harrison. Should we speak to him?'

'You don't need to do that!' I'd look like a raging idiot. I had to tell him the whole story of seeing the ambulance come from the British merchant ship yesterday, seeking out the sick Patrick Harrison here at the hospital and making arrangements for my passage with the ship's officers. It took some time. He kept interrupting me with questions about details that seemed irrelevant.

'The *Trevor* sails at ten.' I was squirming inside and close to tears. My story made me look like a scheming runaway.

Inspector Neuberger glanced at the fob watch chained to his waistcoat and said in a matter-of-fact voice, 'That's barely an hour from now. Are you expecting to make it?'

I looked at the floor and shook my head.

'Good.' His tone was conversational as he wrote. 'Because we don't want you to leave the country right now.'

I *was* a suspect!

I waited while he went through another nose-blowing performance with delicate precision. At the end of it, he sniffed noisily. 'How did your mother feel about your leaving?'

'Why?'

'Why do I want to know this?'

'Yes.'

'I want to establish your mother's state of mind.' He put his notepad down on his knees. 'There is no need to glare at me, Miss Lena Levi. I am only trying to understand what happened. It is possible that...'

'She didn't know.'

'You didn't tell her?' He seemed intent on making me feel bad about myself.

'No.' I looked out of the window. It was an exceptionally starry night. The Milky Way looked like a great white veil dotted with tiny silver beads. It would have been a wonderful night for sailing away. 'I was going to.'

He picked up his pad and started writing again. 'She didn't know you were leaving.'

'I had mentioned something to her about wanting to.'

'I see.'

'What do you see?' I was half pleading, half defiant.

His dark eyes looked world-weary as they met mine. 'It is possible that she wanted to take her own life.'

Later, Dr Rosenblum put his head around the door and told us Mutti was stable. The three of us jumped to our feet. But there was no further news.

'You should go home. Any change tonight is most unlikely.'

I shook my head. 'I can't leave. I feel responsible for her.'

After the doctor left, I told Sara and Dov, 'You go.'

Sara nodded like she understood.

Dov put his hand on my shoulder. 'Here's some money for a cab home, so you won't be stuck.'

We wouldn't want me to be stuck, I thought bitterly, gazing at the coins in my hand. As the door closed slowly behind them, I glowered. This was all Dov's fault for chucking Mutti in favour of Sara.

I sat down and gazed out of the window with my weary head in my hand. A ship was heading out, towards the inky horizon. Smoke from the stack billowed into the night as it ploughed upside down 'Vs' through the water. In no time at all, it had disappeared into the black. It was quarter past ten. No doubt it was the *Trevor*.

I sneaked a pot of tea and two cups I'd wheedled from Mutti's nurse into Patrick Harrison's ward. He was surprised to see me. 'You didn't go?'

'My mother was admitted here,' I whispered.

'What's up with 'er, then?'

'She was shot.'

He gaped at me. 'What a turn up... How is she?'

'We can't say yet.'

I sipped my tea and pulled a face. 'The tea doesn't taste like in England.'

'It never does,' he said. 'Not anywhere, no matter where you roam. But it was a nice thought. So 'ow did your mum get shot?'

'It wasn't my mum!'

'I thought you said...'

'It was my Israeli mother.'

'You have more than one muvver?'

I explained, as briefly as I could, how this had come about.

He lay back on the pillows, shaking his head. 'If that ain't a carry on.' After a moment, he continued, 'You're fortunate having two muvvers. I don't even have one, meself.'

'You don't?'

'I never knew her. She gave me up at birth, ha ha. I'm a Dr Barnardo's boy, I am.' Seeing my look of concern, he was quick to add, 'Aw, don't pity me. There are a lot worse things than growin' up in an orphanage. Look at me, I turned out alright, wouldn't you say? I'm doing what I always wanted, cooking and travel. When I was a little-un, I'd go down the docks to watch the ships and dream of sailing away one day. And, Bob's yer uncle, here I am.'

I laughed. 'With a girl in every port?'

'If only!'

He thought I was flirting with him and maybe I was. He might not be good-looking, but he had charm.

'Seriously though, I have good prospects. I'll be a ship's chef one day. Later on, I might open me own caff.' He winked. 'You could do a lot worse for yerself than take up with Patrick 'Arrison.'

'You're a tonic, Patrick.' I got to my feet. 'You've cheered me up no end.'

'Don't go. Don't go. You didn't tell me yet how your mum, the Israel one I mean, came to be shot.'

'Oh, it was a sniper. She was up on the mountain, guarding the cattle, and a sniper got her.'

I laid my hand on the numbers on Mutti's left arm, willing her eyes to open. Nothing happened. She remained deathly pale and still. I wondered if she would die. I was so sorry she'd had such a terrible life. I couldn't begin to imagine what all the hatred shown her had done to how she saw the world. Her way of seizing any joy available seemed only natural in the circumstances.

Everyone she cared about had abandoned her, starting with the boy she loved, my father. Her parents had coolly sent her off to be that German woman's slave and condemned her to dance in front of drooling Nazis to make ends meet. And Dov had chosen Sara.

She must have had high hopes that her turn for sweetness had finally come when the long-lost daughter chose her. But all I'd done was make it clear I preferred the life I had before. And in the end, I'd told her I wanted to leave her too. How could I have been so heartless?

Well, I'd be her Lena Levi again. 'If You will only restore her to me. Please.' I squeezed her hand. 'Don't die, Mutti. I love you.'

It turned out I couldn't bear to think of life without her.

Chapter Twenty-two

On Day Three of Mutti's hospitalisation, they told us they expected her to pull through. We were still on tenterhooks. We didn't know how bad she would be when she woke up. She might be paralysed. Or a vegetable.

On the morning of Day Six, she opened her eyes. They weren't the doll's eyes we'd been warned about. They had expression.

Although I felt like punching the air, I made myself approach her quietly. 'Imma, you're awake.'

'Lena, you're here,' she murmured, and closed them again. A weight fell from my shoulders. She was herself. It was alright to feel tired now. With a trudging step and a soaring heart, I went out of the hospital and into the clear light of day. I got a cab back to the kibbutz.

In bed in her bungalow, I found I couldn't sleep. I was too excited. The future looked so bright I wanted to walk into it, right then. I had no inkling of all the floor-pacing that still lay ahead of me, through operation after operation. I was grateful to God for answering my prayers and told Him so, over and over. When, finally, I did sleep, I slept right through to the next morning.

A few days after Mutti woke up, Inspector Neuberger took me up to the mountain. This was mainly, I think, because I refused to believe she'd tried to kill herself.

Mutti couldn't speak clearly or for long but she was crystal clear about not knowing what happened when her rifle discharged a bullet on the afternoon of Wednesday, 11th October. 'It must have been an accident. One minute I was clearing out the sukkah, the next I was waking up in hospital.'

The festival of Sukkot – Tabernacles – had finished the week before. We ate all our meals in the sukkah, a booth decorated with fruit and vegetables. Some even slept there. The festival celebrated the harvest and also remembered the hardships the Children of Israel endured in the desert after Moses led them out of slavery in Egypt, the fragility of their lives, and how they were dependent on God for everything. Small wonder Jews still celebrated it. Our lives were just as fragile today.

There was a second sukkah up on the mountain for those who were on guard duty. The inspector and I stood beside it. It was a windy day. His flapping three-piece suit looked out of place up there in the wilds.

He told me that Mutti had, indeed, been given the task of taking down the remaining perishable decorations because they were rotting and attracting swarms of flies and vermin that were a nuisance to everyone in the breeze-block shelter nearby. She was alone. Uri's dad, with whom she was sharing her stint, was checking on the stock that had wandered down the mountain.

She should have been inside the shelter, covering him. She should have waited until he returned before working on the sukkah. 'This is a procedural issue, perhaps irrelevant to the case in hand. But perhaps also significant, if she wanted us to believe in an accident.'

We went inside. Even though the perishable decorations had been removed, the sickly-sweet stench of rotting produce still hung in the air. The inspector kicked with his black leather shoes at a patch of dark dirt. 'This is where your mother fell. Her rifle was found beside her, just here.'

How could he be so matter-of-fact?

'That doesn't prove anything,' I countered. I really wanted it not to be that she'd planned this. 'The rifle could have fallen anywhere. Someone might have moved it.'

Inevitably, he reached into his pockets, all of them in turn. I knew what he was looking for. He looked alarmed at not finding it. I held out the clean hankie I'd taken from my drawer and stuffed into my shorts that morning. I didn't usually need a handkerchief but took it as a precaution: right then, there was no telling when I might find myself blubbering. He took it from me, shook it open with a flick of his hand, like he wanted to produce a dove, blew his nose and took a root around inside his nostrils. After a moment's hesitation, he offered to return it to me.

I shook my head. 'Keep it.'

As he put the hankie into his trouser pocket, I noticed the blue letter 'P' embroidered in the corner. Peter's handkerchief! I felt bereft.

Several minutes had passed and I couldn't remember what we had been talking about.

Inspector Neuberger had not forgotten. 'Where the rifle fell is less important than the fact it had been fired.'

I looked around me at the Arab villages on the surrounding hillsides. A sniper could easily have been hiding on a flat roof or at a window of any one of those houses.

'Perhaps my mother saw something, some danger.' I was certainly convincing myself: a sniper could be watching us right then, just waiting for his opportunity to pull the trigger and murder us.

'If so, she does not remember. She has not mentioned it.'

There had to be an innocent explanation. I racked my brain for one. 'A rabbit for our supper, maybe?'

Though even I thought this a stretch, I was surprised by his reaction. He looked at me like I was nuts. 'If you mean the hyraxes we have here, they are not kosher.'

I experienced an all-too-familiar feeling of not being quite the goods, and all because of what I didn't know.

'We did not find the bullet from her rifle,' he said, 'but that also is not so important. Your mother's injuries were consistent with having been self-inflicted.'

Her cheek and part of her neck had been ripped away. I would show him he was wrong! I would hunt for bullets myself. I would find evidence to establish that she'd meant to fire at someone about to shoot her.

I quickly realised this plan was nothing more than a bid to banish the guilt that was weighing heavily on me. Sooner or later, I would have to accept that I'd made her miserable enough to want to die. Though I felt terrible, I was also furious. What she'd done felt controlling, a huge overreaction. Malicious.

I was busily searching. Inspector Neuberger watched me for a moment. 'I will show you what probably happened.'

He stood by the dark patch of dirt where Mutti had bled and began to act out what followed. 'She placed the butt of the rifle on the ground, leaned in towards the barrel with her mouth wide – like this – and pulled the trigger. Boom! As she did so, the butt slipped, knocking the barrel sideways. Instead of taking off the top of her head and spraying brains everywhere, as she intended, the bullet went through the side of her face.'

I looked on in horror. To my amazement, he wasn't done yet. He threw himself down onto the dirt, twitching and shuddering. I felt woozy. I thought I might throw up. I heard a thud as everything went black.

'What is the matter?' I heard him say, as from a great distance. 'Are you alright?'

When I came to, I found myself in a heap on the ground. The inspector was on his knees beside me, waving his arms and looking concerned.

As Mutti went down for one of her successive operations, I walked up from the Rambam to Stella Maris, a century-old church attached to a Carmelite monastery. Inside were walls like sugar frosting and a dark cave that the monks maintained was where the prophet Elijah once lived.

It felt like a good place to pray. I was praying all the time now, mainly for Mutti to be restored to full health. At Stella Maris, I prayed that she'd come through today's operation alright. The more I prayed, the better I felt. I knew I didn't have to fret about things because God was looking after them for me. Even so, after I came out, I kept having to remind myself of it.

The bright sun was piercing through the clouds following a surprise cloudburst that had left the road glistening and a smell of wet dust in the air. Above the cliff edge where I stood facing the sweeping bay, a huge rainbow curved across the sky. Everything looked good and beautiful. It felt like a sign.

I started down the steep path lined with ruins of stepped terraces from who could say when. They may have been growing things there in biblical times. At the bottom, close to the shore, beside a different cave, which rabbis claimed to be that of Elijah, I spotted a road sign to Atlit. Atlit was where Mutti had been imprisoned by the British when she first arrived in Israel after the war.

Sitting with her earlier that week in the hospital, she had told me how she and all the other detainees had escaped. 'There was a rumour going around that the British soldiers who ran the place were planning to deport us.' When she talked, it was like she had a gobstopper in her mouth. The doctors hoped that would reduce, or even disappear, over time. 'So Palmach decided to help us escape.'

'What's that?'

'The Jewish Secret Army.'

'Ah, the Israelis.'

'You can't call them that. This was before the Independence.' Mutti lay back against the pillows and closed her eyes. 'Don't make me talk too much. It makes me dizzy.' She was the one who'd decided to start telling a story. But I held back from being snarky. She was, after all, an invalid.

'Where was I?' She was suddenly wide awake again. '*Ja*, people from Palmach posed as instructors for the courses the British organised to keep us occupied. As well as teaching us classes, they also broke the firing pins of the guns the British had issued the Arab guards they'd hired.' She giggled. 'The escape was on a moonless night when the guards couldn't see them approaching. When the Arabs finally saw they were under attack, they found they couldn't shoot the attackers!' Her eyes widened. 'We prisoners had no idea it was going to happen. I was having a quiet cigarette in the courtyard when suddenly there were my Hebrew teacher and my English teacher, rounding up the guards who'd surrendered. They gave me a gun and told me to watch them while they gathered the detainees together.'

'Did you know how to use it?'

'I knew to pull the trigger.' She flicked a dismissive wrist. 'It was enough.'

There was something about the picture I had of Mutti, taken by surprise yet coming through as a guard, that I found intensely exciting. 'Did they behave, your Arab prisoners?'

'Lena, too many questions!'

'What about the British soldiers? Where were they?'

She snorted and then shook her head at me. 'Ach! They were sleeping.' She placed a finger to her lips. 'That was why we all had to be silent... Know what was funny?'

I leaned forward to find out. 'What?'

'We prisoners refused to be rescued without our treasures. Palmach thought we were *meshugenahs*. They didn't understand that these were little items we'd all managed to keep through hiding, through the camps and through the journey here. Through it all.

'I had a little picture of you with Rifka and Lottie in Rifka's garden. It had been everywhere with me in my underwear. I wasn't going without that.'

I frowned at her. 'So, where is it?'

'In my bedside table drawer at home.'

Didn't she understand that a picture like that would be important to me? 'Why haven't you shown it to me?'

She waved a hand. 'Ach! I have you for real now. The picture is nothing. Don't keep interrupting, Lena.'

'Please do go on.' My voice was sugar-sweet. I adopted an exaggerated listening pose.

'After a big discussion they had to let us go and get our things. But then the British started to wake up! We had to run for the trucks the Palmach people had brought. My heart was going thump-thump-thump.' She was talking now as if she was breathless. 'But we made it. After a few miles, the trucks stopped. They ordered us out and let the trucks go ahead to fool the British. Meanwhile we set off on foot, up Mount Carmel. Remember, it was a moonless night? No one could see anything. It was hard work. Everyone was stumbling on the stony path.

'I was carrying a little girl on my shoulders. She could have been you. I was thinking about you then and hoping that whoever had you at that moment was looking after you well for me.'

I wasn't convinced she really had thought of me. But she knew how to make a good story. I took her hand and squeezed it, regardless.

'We walked all night. It was almost morning by the time we reached Kibbutz Beit Oren at the top of Mount Carmel. But we couldn't stay there. It was well known as a Palmach place. Kibbutz Eshkadosh didn't have that reputation. So, after a drink of water and a short rest, we carried on, over the top and down the other side, until we got there.'

'You must have been exhausted.'

'*Ja*, I was. *Total kaputt*. Someone else had to carry the little girl. It was all I could do to lift one foot after the other.' She fell silent and closed her eyes again.

'And the British didn't find you?'

'I haven't finished.' She opened her eyes wide and stared, as if to show me she hadn't just dozed off. 'I was only remembering it all. It was a fantastic escape.'

A slow smile lit up her half-bandaged face. 'That morning, word went out all over Haifa about what had happened. Do you know what? Thousands of Jews walked out to Kibbutz Eshkadosh, all the way from the city. They made a big crowd that mingled with those of us who'd escaped so that when the British came, they could not tell who was prisoner and who was not.'

I laughed in delight at this and so did Mutti.

'And that is how I got to be a kibbutznik at Kibbutz Eshkadosh.'

That evening, when I returned to our bungalow, I went straight to Mutti's bedside table. The photo was tiny, no more than three inches square. It was veined and crumpled. Three figures faced the camera – an adult, a girl and a toddler – but their features were blurred. I would never have known myself, or them. Nothing about the picture rang any bells. What a disappointment! It was strange that Mutti took such risks to keep it.

The signpost – an old black and white one, identical to those we had back home – indicated that Atlit was only ten miles away. I turned around to take in the steep path I'd just descended from Stella Maris, wondering whether it might have been the very one Mutti and the escaping prisoners climbed.

I crossed the road to the sea and walked back along the shore towards the hospital, mulling over why Mutti would keep a photo of unrecognisable people. Maybe it was the occasion that was important, the four of us together – I presumed she was the photographer for, surely, she'd have been in it with us, otherwise? Maybe it was worth everything to remind yourself there could be days that were sweet when all of life was bitter.

Almost at the Rambam, I left the coastline to follow HaAliya HaShniya Street, which was busy with early evening shoppers buying what they needed for supper – if they could get it. With so many people pouring into the country, food was sometimes in short supply. And people in this street, and everywhere else I'd been in Haifa, didn't seem to have much money.

It was quite something that such folk, hearing of the detainees' escape from Atlit, had laid aside their plans – and wages – for the day to help. They had gone up to Kibbutz Eshkadosh to stand in solidarity with Mutti and the others to save them from recapture and deportation. That made me proud to be Israeli.

Chapter Twenty-three

The week before Mutti was discharged, Patrick Harrison came with me to visit her. He and the *Trevor* were back in Haifa. His constant flow of jokes made Mutti laugh. She liked him a lot but commented – thankfully not to his face – that it was a shame he was so ugly. I had to smile. She was no picture book herself. One cheek was two-tone where they had performed plastic surgery, and she had a ragged scar down the side of her jaw.

Patrick and I went for a stroll around Haifa. He was like a boisterous puppy with too much energy. I liked him better when he was sick. I didn't expect to see him again. So, I seized the opportunity to go on board with him and apologise to the captain and the cook for letting them down. They were very kind about it.

We had tea and biscuits in the galley. It was good to drink English tea and talk with English people. They asked me all about Mutti's accident. I skirted around telling them details. They wished her a speedy recovery and me happiness in my new life as an Israeli, for which I thanked them with a smile.

Getting up from that little table in the ship's galley to return to shore felt like I was leaving home behind me all over again. I was filled with sadness. Patrick came to the gangplank to say goodbye. He wanted a kiss, but all he got was a peck on the cheek. My heart still belonged to Peter Price, even if he belonged to Babs.

I squeezed into a crowded *sherut* to travel back to the kibbutz. It smelled of things virtually unknown on English public transport – garlic and sweat and a kind of farm smell. I looked out of the window and thought about how Peter and I became friends, talking over the garden fence. As we travelled through streets lined with dusty merchants in Middle Eastern clothing, loudly touting watermelons and fresh nuts, I was taken back to Canterbury, and our 'first date'. I was twelve.

I had on a flouncy summer dress that Mum had sewn for me. It had required an extravagant amount of yellow cotton and coupons – clothing was still rationed. He wore his grey school shorts and blazer.

We went to see where his old house was, close to the ancient turrets of the entrance to St Augustine's Abbey and a small green.

'Here it is,' Peter said with a flourish, like a lord revealing his domain. Before us was a gravelled car park, lined with shrubs – the inevitable purple buddleia, and pink willowherb, both on their way out, since this was September.

'This is where you lived?' It was hard to imagine houses here. 'What was it like?'

'It was just an old cottage overlooking...' He turned with another flourish.

Behind us was the city wall, and behind that the cathedral with its high tower and pointy bits. This would have been a nice place to live, I thought, with quite a bit more character than the thirties' builds of Lanfranc Close.

'It was quaint, snug, cramped – a medieval house in a row of medieval houses, doing no one any harm.' His face became solemn. 'Home.'

On the night of 1st June 1942, Peter's family sat cramped in their cellar, listening to anti-aircraft guns and the whistle of bombs falling. 'They shook the earth as they exploded.' He grabbed at a stalk of willowherb and began punctuating his words by hitting it against his leg. 'They were getting louder and closer.'

'I bet you were scared.'

'I spent the time trying to tell which bombers they were—Dorniers or Heinkels, Junkers 88s or Messerschmitts.'

I laughed. That sounded about right for Peter.

Eventually, everything went quiet. Peter's family sat in almost total darkness. The power had gone out. Their only light was an old hurricane lamp that was short of fuel. They never did hear the all-clear. They smelled smoke…

'It was getting bad. We were coughing. Dad went upstairs to investigate and came right back, saying the house was on fire! We got out quick.'

He described how everything outside was strange. The ground was littered with their possessions and broken glass from their windows. The city was lit up with fierce flames and the spray of fire hoses. Walls were tumbling.

'We traipsed through hot streets, unsure of our geography. Little bits of burning paper were floating around us like butterflies.' There was a choke in Peter's voice as he went on. 'I couldn't believe it. We were homeless.'

I wanted to console him with a hug. Of course, I didn't. 'But you have a home now,' was the lame comfort I offered.

They went to the station and waited for the first train to Tenterden, where Peter's auntie lived. All they had was the small bag that Mrs Price always took into the cellar with them when there were air raids. They didn't come back to live in Canterbury, in Lanfranc Close, for four years.

After our visit, we went for the little, round ice creams wrapped in greaseproof paper that an elderly lady would sell. All the children knew her because ice cream was so hard to come by then. We had to rush, or they'd all be gone.

My *sherut* stopped to let people off at the industrial area of Check Post, with its many factories. The Technion Institute of Technology looked like a Turkish palace, sitting on the hill, up to my right. We were almost at the open countryside that led to the kibbutz.

While Peter was losing his home and Canterbury was being flattened, I was safely tucked up in the folds of the Welsh hills, miles away from all the bombs. My war experience had been cotton wool compared to his.

Chapter Twenty-four

Christmas Day in Israel was just like any other working day. The Jewish nation didn't celebrate the birth of Jesus, which seemed weird. After all, this was His country.

There was one festive aspect to Haifa. Many of the balconies belonging to Christian Arabs that Dov and I were passing along HaGefen Street were decorated with Santa Claus and his reindeer, or snow scenes. We were bringing Mutti home which made it a very special Christmas.

And today was my fifteenth birthday. No one seemed to have noticed, which was alright: Mutti coming home was the best present I could have wished for.

She was still very weak from all the operations, and more plastic surgery lay ahead. At least for now, there would be no more agonising over gaping wounds and hanging flesh that might get infected.

She still talked a bit funny, although that was improving, and she looked drunk when she walked because her balance had been affected, but it could have been so much worse. The bullet had passed close to her spinal cord. If that had been severed, she would have been paralysed. Above all, her mind was intact. Even if, for now, she sat subdued in the back of the jeep, I was confident her sparkle would return eventually.

As we drove through the gates of Kibbutz Eshkadosh, everyone dropped what they were doing to welcome Mutti home. We drove past smiling faces to the quadrangle. Everyone was cheering and applauding. Dov turned back to wink at Mutti as the crowd, having circled around to greet her personally, gradually began to drift away. No doubt, she would enjoy a good cup of real coffee, he suggested.

'Ken.' She nodded.

My heart sank. It seemed like they shared a secret. Surely the two of them weren't starting up again? Dov headed for the hut that was our office-cum-café, leaving me to guide Mutti there after him, slowly. Despite her stick, she leaned heavily on me as we went.

Sara came up to us. 'We're glad you're home, Rochel.'

'Me too.' Mutti said. *'Mazal tov.'*

'Thank you.' Sara smiled a proper smile. I didn't know she could do that.

'*Mazal tov*?' I said.

'Sara and Dov are getting married,' Mutti said.

'I didn't know.'

'Now you do.'

I turned to Sara. 'Congratulations.'

We shared a hug. It was at my instigation and it was lukewarm. But it was a hug, nevertheless, and felt like a huge step towards friendship.

Sara turned to Mutti, who wobbled on her feet.

'You are good for him.' Mutti pinched her cheek. After a moment's hesitation, they hugged too.

Inside, Dov already had the kettle on and was laying out cups on the table with the yellow Formica counter that reminded me of our kitchen at home. Today there'd be a stuffed bird in the oven; a tree in the living room; streets, damp and silent; and chilly weather, perhaps even snow. A place far away in time and distance. Real life to me now was here, in Israel, in a short-sleeved shirt and cotton skirt, surrounded by ginger hills.

There was a package on the counter. It was wrapped in Christmas paper – Santas with long, white beards on a red background. They made the warm sunlight streaming through the windows seem out of place. In reality, of course, it was the Christmas present that was the oddity.

'Is that for me?'

Mutti and Dov grinned at one another.

Mutti took a sudden interest in her fingernails. 'I know nothing about it.'

'You should open it,' Dov said.

The present was rectangular. The writing on the label that dangled from the strings was familiar: 'To Darling Marlene, Merry Christmas and Happy Birthday, Love Mum xx'.

'You've been hoarding my mail?'

'It came to me direct,' Dov put up his hands. 'Along with a request to make sure you got it on the right day.'

'Happy Birthday, *schatzi*.' Mutti clasped her hands together. 'Now, open it. I want to see what's inside.' As I tore off the wrappings, she asked, 'Is it shoes?'

The box I uncovered was indeed a shoebox, but no shoes were inside. I lifted the lid and my hands flew to my mouth. There, surrounded by white tissue paper, lay One-Eyed Lottie, looking up at me with love in her eye.

'Ach, *Du liebe Zeit*,' Mutti exclaimed. '*Die kleine Puppe ist wieder wohl geworden*!'

She was right. My little doll was all mended and in one piece again. It was like seeing a corpse revived. I picked her up. She was cleaner and altogether plumper than before, but her good eye was still her eye, her mouth was still her mouth, her hair was still her hair, and she still had on her red woollen pinafore. I wondered how Mum had pulled this off. It must have taken her weeks.

Buzzing with the thrill of having Lottie back, I hugged her to me. 'She's quite the traveller – Germany, England and now Israel.' I was laughing as I sat her on my lap and waggled her arms, like I surely did when I was small.

Dov brought a plate of almond biscuits with what turned out to be instant coffee. 'Something else.' He laid an envelope on the table beside my cup. It was Mum's writing on that too. It said, 'Marlene.'

Inside was a card. It was a bit juvenile perhaps but appropriate, since it featured a cartoon of a little girl in a hat, lifting her doll from a chair. The caption at the top read, 'Happy Birthday, *young lady*!'

It was a sweet card. There was also a letter. I was expecting Mum's usual blah, but this was different, right from the first line. The part that really got my attention was when she said that she'd been remembering every day how I came to be her daughter:

> *After applying to the Home Office and being accepted, we heard nothing for what seemed a long time.*

Dad and I knew children were coming in, but we weren't contacted. The waiting was terrible.

It was June 1939 before we were finally asked to come and meet you at Southampton docks. We thought this was odd because all the other children had come to Liverpool Street railway station in London. It turned out your boat was the only one to come direct from Germany.

It took us forever to get there from Wales. When we finally arrived, we saw hordes of children, all chattering like starlings in German and drinking soup from mugs. Each of you had a numbered, brown tag on your front. You looked like parcels.

Well, I thought we'd never find you in all this confusion. Just then they called our name over the loudspeaker system. We went to the desk and there you were, an enchanting little dark berry of a girl with Lottie tucked under your arm.

You turned out to be just three years old, though someone had put you down as five.

I glanced up at Mutti who was smiling in her new, wonky way. What could she have been thinking, sending me away all alone when I was so small?

You looked up at us with those juicy eyes of yours and gave me your little hand. Our hearts melted. We took you home.

I thought my own heart would melt.

Marlene, I've never regretted it, not a single day. To me, you were my own daughter from the start and that has been my downfall. I so wanted it to be true that I convinced myself and hid who you really were from you. That was wrong and I am sorry. I hope you can forgive me.

I put my nose down to the table, cradled my head in my arms, and there, in my kind of nest, I had a jolly good cry. When I'd finished, I lifted my head again to see the stunned faces of Mutti and Dov.

'It's alright.' I wiped my eyes. 'I'm crying because I'm happy.'

The pain that flashed across Mutti's face sent an arrow of anxiety through me that left me wondering whether she might try to take her life again.

Chapter Twenty-five

I'd set out before to visit Rabbi Shlomo Liebermann but hadn't got there. This time, however, I needed advice and didn't know who else to turn to. He opened the door and blinked at me. His hair was tousled, and I wondered for a moment whether he'd just got out of bed. Then I remembered he'd looked a bit like that before, when we were on the ship.

'Shalom, Rabbi.' I saved myself just in time from doing the handshake thing. I now knew that Orthodox Jews didn't shake hands with women because they might be having their period.

A smile spread across his face, which was as hairy as ever. He stood back from the doorway to let me into the narrow hallway.

He showed me into his little living room, which was dark and dusty. The blinds were down, shutting out the slanting January afternoon sun, which I'd watched throw diamonds across the sea as I walked along his road.

There were a lot of books on shelves around the walls. On the dining table was a large, ornate Hebrew Bible, open at the story of the parting of the Red Sea in the book of Exodus. Decorating the centre of the table was a crocheted white doily, a curiously feminine touch in his male world. There was an odd, pervasive smell I couldn't place at first. Then I realised what it was – cabbage.

He bumbled in after me with a glass of water, which he put on the low coffee table, and motioned for me to sit behind it on the threadbare sofa against the wall. He sat on an upright chair by the dining table and drummed his fingers on the buttons stretched across his round belly. His shirt, like the sofa, had seen better days. It was tinged yellow, like his teeth, and the collar was frayed.

'It is good to see you again, Miss Lena Levi,' he said with a grin. I was amazed he remembered my name. It had been more than six months. 'How are you doing?'

I opened my mouth to reply, but couldn't find any words, so I shrugged.

A half-mocking twinkle came to his eye. '*Nu,* we could discuss the level of the water in the Sea of Galilee. Or we could get straight down to why you have come to see me.'

'I thought maybe you could help me clear my thoughts.' I took a sip of water and launched in. 'The thing is, I can't be in two places at once, but that is what is happening and it's tearing me apart. I'm here, but my thoughts are always *there*.'

'Where is *there*?'

'Home.'

'I see. You know that it is the same for everyone? We are all now somewhere else. But this is the Land HaShem promised us.' He jabbed a finger towards the ceiling, indicating God. 'A land flowing with milk and honey, our Jewish homeland.'

'Mutti says Israel stands for hope and I feel that too. I want to be a pioneer and help build this nation. I've set out to make Israel my home, but I'm failing.'

I couldn't bear to think of myself as someone who just gave up, but if my main reason for staying was pride in the kind of person I was, that didn't feel right. And that seemed to be the case. That and Mutti being so needy.

'I still feel like an outsider.' A wedge of self-pity lodged itself in my throat. 'And it's like I'm in a prison all the time.'

I expected him to speak, but he only nodded. So, I went on, 'I can't leave, anyway. I can't just leave Mutti. She had an accident, you see, though she's back on her feet now and milking cows again – slowly. But she spent all my money – Mum's money. So, I am stuck.'

The rabbi drummed his fingers some more. 'This is a lot to take in.'

'The worst part of it is I miss my mum really badly. I didn't think she loved me, but now I know she does.'

'Isn't she here with you?'

'No, that's Mutti.'

'I see.' He looked like he didn't see at all.

'Mum and Mutti are two different people.'

'You have two mothers?'

I had to explain my situation to the rabbi. He nodded as I spoke. Afterwards, he was silent for some time, his eyes closed. I wondered if he had fallen asleep.

But no. He cleared his throat. 'Let us look to the Tanach, the Bible. We have the story about Shlomo, which is my own name. You call him Solomon, I think. He was a very wise man, like me. He had to judge between two women who both claimed to be a baby's mother.'

'I hate that story. It's gruesome.'

'The real mother was willing to give up the child so that it would live.'

I sighed. 'Mutti doesn't seem willing to give me up.'

'Ah,' he said. 'But the life of the baby who was going to be cut in half was in danger. That's not your situation. Is it?'

He had a point. 'No.'

'So, let us look to other stories in the Tanach for the answer. On the one hand, we have Ruth. She stayed close to her mother-in-law when she came into the Land of Israel, even promising she would stay with her to the grave. On the other hand, we have Daniel. After he was carried off to Babylon, he stayed among the goyim and helped them his whole life, which he lived out in exile.'

He seemed to be weighing the pros and cons of staying in Israel or leaving. But there was a bit more to my problem than that.

'On the other hand…'

Did he have three hands?

'… there is the story of Ancel.'

I wasn't familiar with that one. 'Er, who?'

The rabbi's features softened as his voice grew softer too. 'Ancel is my son. He was only thirteen in the summer of 1941, when I decided to leave him in a monastery. The brothers took him in. It was a good decision. Things were never good for Jews in Hungary and, in March 1944, when the Germans marched in, they began mass deportations of Jews, mostly to Auschwitz-Birkenau. Most were killed as soon as they got there.'

'Mutti was in Auschwitz.'

'*Baruch* HaShem that she survived that terrible killing factory. More than a million were murdered there.'

'How did you survive?'

A grin spread across his face. 'I was with the partisans in the mountains. It was dangerous. No one knew if they would survive the day.' His eyes went around the stuffy little room where we were sitting. 'That was what made it so exciting.

'I wasn't able to return for Ancel until late in 1945. I hadn't seen my son for more than four years. I went up to the monastery that was like a great castle from olden times and knocked on the great wooden door, only to learn that Ancel had become a novice monk. The last time I saw him, he was dressed in a long black dress with a cross around his neck!'

Rabbi Liebermann looked grief-stricken. My heart went out to him.

'He is a Christian, Lena. A Christian. He has taken monastic orders. He'd like to come to Israel and see it. He has the heart that I gave to him for the Land. We talked about it when we sat at home and when we walked by the way, when we lay down and when we got up, like it says in Torah. But he is Brother Benedict today and he goes where they tell him to.'

I looked on, helpless, as he struggled to regain his composure.

'I am sad that he does not love his Judaism as I do,' he said. 'But I am happy, so very happy, my son is not scattered bones today. What I chose for Ancel was the right choice. He lives.' He closed his eyes for a moment. When he opened them again, he looked tired and drawn. 'As for what he has chosen for himself, *nu*, I was no longer there to point him in the direction I hoped he'd go. And he has chosen what he has chosen.' He cleared his throat and beamed at me. 'I hope that helps?'

It was plain that our conversation was at a close. I got to my feet. 'Thank you,' I said, although nothing was any clearer. All he'd done was talk about himself.

Alone in the bungalow that evening, before Mutti came home, I read about King Solomon's wise judgement in my Bible. I hoped she wouldn't come in and find me reading this story. It would only lead to questions.

This is how the Bible story went:

Two pregnant women lived in the same house and had babies within three days of one another. Nobody else was around when this happened.

One woman told the king, 'One night, while we were asleep, the other mother rolled over on top of her baby and he died. While I was sleeping, she swapped the babies. She took my son from beside me in my bed and put him in her bed. Then she put her dead baby in beside me. When I got up to feed my son the next morning, I found him dead! Then it got light and I could see he wasn't my son.'

'That's not so!' the second woman cried. 'He was your son. My son is alive!'

'Yours is the dead baby,' the first woman screamed. 'Mine is alive!'

Solomon could hardly get a word in edgeways. 'Since you both say the living baby is yours, I need someone to get me a sword.'

A sword was brought. Solomon ordered, 'Cut the baby up and give each mother half.'

The baby's mother stepped forward. 'Please, don't kill my son. Your Majesty, I love him very much; give him to her rather than kill him.'

The other woman didn't care. She agreed to Solomon's judgement.

'Don't hurt the baby.' Solomon pointed to the first woman. 'She is the rightful mother. Let her have him.'

The true mother loved her child enough to give him up. I didn't think that would be the case with Mutti.

Chapter Twenty-six

I thought a lot about Solomon and about Rabbi Liebermann's son, Ancel, in the days that followed, during breaktime at school or when I flopped on my bed after a stint looking after the tinies.

Sometimes I'd look up from doing my homework and float away to a castle monastery somewhere in Hungary. Ancel had accepted Jesus as his Messiah. No doubt his father thought that the monks had corrupted him. In the eyes of any Jew, Ancel and I had made ourselves outcasts by being Christian. We had crossed a line that made us traitors. This seemed unfair. In my case, I hadn't even known that I was Jewish until Mutti came and claimed me.

Even after seven months of living here, I still didn't feel very Jewish. In fact, here in Jesus' homeland, I was feeling daily more Christian. His presence was everywhere. He had buoyed me up through my darkest days.

My faith alienated me from others on the kibbutz, even more than my English ways. I longed to just be myself: go to church, drink tea with Mum...

In the Solomon story, I'd thought the real mother could only be the natural mother. But it was the one who loved the child enough to let her go that Solomon deemed the real mother. In my story, that was Mum.

It took me a whole lot more thinking to realise that when the life of her daughter was in danger, Mutti had done that too. She had loved me enough to give me up to strangers.

It came to me eventually that the rabbi's words – 'What I chose for Ancel was the right choice. He lives' – would be the place to begin with Mutti.

I waited until Shabbat morning. Mutti was in a good mood. She had sung *Bab el Wad* to the kibbutz the previous night, her first time since the accident – or rather, since she tried to take her life. It was truth time.

The sun was shining and the sky was blue. I suggested we eat breakfast outside on the porch of our bungalow. We helped ourselves to rolls and coffee in the canteen and took them back with us.

I was more than a little nervous. I didn't know how this would turn out. I picked my words carefully. 'Mutti, what you chose for me – when you sent me to England – was the right choice. I would not be alive today if you hadn't done that.'

She smiled and nodded approvingly, basking in my compliment.

I hesitated, not knowing quite where to go next. And then I remembered more of what Rabbi Liebermann had said about his son. Golly, he had helped me far more than I had realised.

'Sadly, you weren't able to bring me up the way you would have wanted. I haven't turned out a German Jewish girl like you. Or even an Israeli, which I've been playing at being ever since I got here. I'm different from the way you might have hoped. It's not your fault and it's not mine. The world got in the way.'

By now, Mutti realised something was up. I had never spoken to her this way before. Or to anyone. She was sitting up straight, all attention, and her face was anxious. 'What are you saying, Lena?'

'I have chosen what I have chosen because of the way I've been brought up.'

I wasn't volatile and haphazard like her. I was steady and predictable, like Mum. I was a Christian because I'd had the opportunity to learn about Jesus, which I would not otherwise have had. Just like Ancel.

Her eyes narrowed. 'What have you chosen?'

'I'm going home.'

'No, you're not!'

'I am, Mutti.' I was quietly resolute. 'I'm not running away and it's not forever. You will always be in my life. We will always be spending time together.'

'No, no, no! You're *my* daughter!'

'I don't belong to you, I belong to myself.'

'This is a punishment. I haven't been a good mother. I cannot help it. I am who I am.'

'So am I.'

The tears welling in her eyes overflowed and poured down her cheeks. I was so sorry to be the cause of her pain. I reached for her hand. 'I love you, Mutti.'

She snatched it away, sending the roll on her plate flying. 'Leave me alone!'

We sat for some time without speaking, as the birds in the trees around the quadrangle sang. She wiped her eyes with her hands. 'How will I ever manage without you?'

'I suppose the same way as you managed before.'

'How will you go?'

I had no idea. 'I'll find a way.'

I breathed a huge sigh of relief as I returned our plates and cutlery to the canteen, not only because I'd said what I had to say, but because Mutti hadn't used her ultimate weapon. She hadn't threatened to kill herself.

By the time I returned, she looked brighter. 'Look,' she said, holding out her mother's bracelet. The string of diamonds set in gold sparkled in the sunlight. 'You can sell this to pay your fare.'

'Oh no, Mutti. I intend to be wearing that on my wedding day, if ever I get married.'

I was deeply touched by her offer. I knew how much she herself treasured that reminder of her family. She grinned. 'I will be there, at your wedding, of course.'

I nodded enthusiastically, hoping that the lump rising in my throat would not turn to tears.

Mutti chewed her lip. She looked as if she wanted to say something, but the words wouldn't come out. Around the quadrangle, scarlet anemones fluttered their petals in the morning breeze. Spring came early to Israel.

Eventually, she spoke. 'Thank you.'

That was unexpected. 'Why?'

'For being my daughter and showing me love.'

Now my tears spilled over. 'I will miss you more than you will ever know.'

'I know what missing feels like,' she said.

We hugged, glued together on the steps of her bungalow.

Chapter Twenty-seven

The captain and cook of the *Trevor* let me work my passage in the galley, though no one gave me much to do and Patrick Harrison kept taking over chopping my vegetables or washing up for me. The captain gave me his own room, as I was the only female on board. My quarters felt very grand.

Our destination was Southampton, the same port where I had first arrived in England from Bremen, a little German Jewish girl with Lottie tucked under my arm.

Now, here I was again, twelve years on, shivering in the biting March wind and loving it because England was looming large: grey docks with grey Southampton buildings behind them under grey skies, and me – a young Englishwoman in high heels from Tel Aviv – thrilled by it all. I was coming home.

I had brought Lottie up on deck with me. She was my connection to Mutti and to Mum, who'd restored her. I felt new and whole, like she was. I was embarking on a new stage in my life, on familiar terrain this time, and I couldn't wait to start.

I leaned into the railings, feeling heady from the swell of the water beneath me, hoping to catch a glimpse of Mum on the distant quay. But cargo ships are not like cruise liners. They don't attract a crowd of well-wishers. Eventually, I had to accept that the *Trevor* hadn't attracted anyone but port officials and Customs officers, and even they weren't stopping what they were doing to watch us dock.

All my joy and anticipation fell away. I became detached, coldly watching myself from outside of my body as I collected my case and joined the rest of the crew in the galley, waiting for the Customs officers who came aboard to inspect us.

After immigration, I said my thank yous and goodbyes, especially to Patrick Harrison, who I knew still wanted to be more than friends, though he'd been a perfect gentleman all the way here.

I went down the gangplank to the quay. No one was in sight. It seemed Mum hadn't come. She came when I was three. But not today. Then I spotted someone standing beyond the port authority barrier – a tall young man. He waved when he saw me. It was Peter! That put a spring in my step.

When I came level with him, I stood my suitcase on the ground and looked up. 'My, you have grown.' He grinned at me, hands stuffed into his pockets. 'Peter, what are you doing here?'

'I thought I'd come and meet you.'

'What about Babs?' I could have bitten my tongue. How uncool was I?

'Who?' He looked puzzled. 'Do you mean your friend from school?'

'Of course.'

'I don't know. Was she coming to meet you?'

I launched myself at him and hugged him hard, which took him by surprise, I think. He caught on, though, and hugged me back. Sort of.

To think that all that time, I'd thought he and Babs... Boy, was I happy now! I was only missing one thing to make my joy complete. I looked around, but there was no sign of her. 'Did Mum come?'

'Of course. She's over there.' He pointed in the direction of the ladies' lavatory. 'She went to wash her face. She couldn't stop herself from crying. "Tears of joy," she said.'

And then there she was, coming towards me in a fashionable new lavender suit with a fitted skirt, and a new hairstyle that was short and wavy.

I galloped towards her and we threw our arms around one another. We hugged for the longest time, both of us sobbing, Mum declaring in my damp ear how happy she was, and me telling her how beautiful she looked, Daddy-O.

Now I really was home.

Find out more about the world of Lena Levi at
beinglenalevi.com.

Resources

General Note

All transliterations of foreign words are the author's own spelling.

Chapters Three and Twenty-five

References to King Solomon and his judgement between two mothers claiming one baby are inspired by the Bible story to be found in 1 Kings 3:16-28.

Chapter Three

Accounts of Jesus' temptation in the desert are found in the Gospels of Matthew, Mark and Luke (Matthew 4:1-11; Mark 1:12-13; Luke 4:1-13): following His baptism by John the Baptist, Jesus fasted for forty days and nights in the Judean Desert of southern Israel, where Satan tried unsuccessfully to tempt him.

King David, as a shepherd boy, equipped himself to take on and overcome the giant Goliath (1 Samuel 17:1-51).

Chapter Six

The Movement for the Care of Children in Germany 1938-1939 was 'a British organization involved in the creation and structuring of Kindertransports, which allowed some Jewish children to enter Britain during 1938 and 1939. The organization appealed to the British parliament ... in order to procure the possibility for children's immigration to England' (source: Los Angeles Museum of the Holocaust: http://www.lamoth.info/?p=creators/creator&id=1552). See also the Jewish Virtual Library (https://www.jewishvirtuallibrary.org/the-kindertransport) and the National Archives' pages on Kindertransport (http://www.nationalarchives.gov.uk/education/resources/kindertransport/) (all accessed 15th February 2019). The Movement for the Care of Children was later known as the Refugee Children's Movement (RCM).

Chapter Seven

The quotation, 'If you prick us, do we not bleed? if you tickle us, do we not laugh? if you poison us, do we not die? and if you wrong us, shall we not revenge?' is from Act 3, Scene 1, of William Shakespeare's play *The Merchant of Venice.* This play can be found at http://shakespeare.mit.edu/merchant/full.html (accessed 15th February 2019).

A reference to the Jewish Agency means the Jewish Agency for Israel, founded in 1929 to link the Jewish state and Jewish communities worldwide. 'The Jewish Agency continues to be the Jewish world's first responder, prepared to address emergencies in Israel, and to rescue Jews from countries where they are at risk.' (Source: http://www.jewishagency.org/inside-jewish-agency/content/4916, accessed 15th February 2019).

Chapter Sixteen

The Central British Fund for Relief and Rehabilitation, originally known as the Central British Fund for German Jewry, was founded in 1933 by Jewish leaders in Britain to help German Jews leave Hitler's Germany for Britain or Israel, then known as Palestine. It was merged with two American groups in 1936 and became the Central Council for Jewish Refugees, supporting refugees in Britain during the Second World War. Since the war, the Central British Fund for Relief and Rehabilitation has focused on the needs of displaced persons.
(Source:
https://archiveshub.jisc.ac.uk/search/archives/e7465947-1e05-3822-a9e7-b9e1ca6128ec, accessed 16th May 2019).

Chapter Twenty-four

Most Kindertransport children arrived at Harwich and were met by their foster families at Liverpool Street Station. However, the steamship *Europa* travelled direct from Bremen and Hamburg to dock in Southampton on 12/13th June 1939.

(Source:
https://www.ushmm.org/online/hsv/source_view.php?SourceId=40228, accessed 16th May 2019).

Chapter Twenty-five

Israel is referred to as 'a land flowing with milk and honey' many times in the Bible's Old Testament, starting with Exodus 3:17. Version quoted here is NIV UK 2011.